"Get me out of here! Please!"

Judy gave him no chance to hang back. She threw the train of her gown over one arm and pulled him into the hall.

"This way," he said. He could at least take her home. She was in no state to face the crowd of wedding guests. She looked like a child caught playing grown-up in somebody's bridal gown. "Take off that veil," he said softly.

She snatched the veil off and flung it to the floor. "I'm sorry. It was awful of me to grab you like I did. I just wanted to get out of there, and you came in…" Her gaze sharpened, taking in his formal attire. "You were to be in the wedding! You were going to be the best man!"

Jake nodded. "Shall I take you home?"

"No!" She wasn't ready to face all the recriminations. "I don't want to go home…."

Eva Rutland began writing when her four children, now all successful professionals, were growing up. Eva lives in California with her husband, Bill, who actively supports and encourages her writing career.

Books by Eva Rutland

HARLEQUIN ROMANCE
2897—TO LOVE THEM ALL
2944—AT FIRST SIGHT
3064—NO ACCOUNTING FOR LOVE
3240—ALWAYS CHRISTMAS
3283—FOREIGN AFFAIR
3412—PRIVATE DANCER
3439—MARRIAGE BAIT

Eva Rutland takes a humorous look at reasons to say "I do!" in this delightful sequel to *Marriage Bait*.

Look out for the follow-up story,
The Million-Dollar Marriage #3518, coming in August.

The Wedding Trap
Eva Rutland

Harlequin Books

TORONTO • NEW YORK • LONDON
AMSTERDAM • PARIS • SYDNEY • HAMBURG
STOCKHOLM • ATHENS • TOKYO • MILAN
MADRID • WARSAW • BUDAPEST • AUCKLAND

ISBN 0-373-03490-3

THE WEDDING TRAP

First North American Publication 1998.

PROLOGUE

JUDITH'S throat was dry. She took a sip of the fresh orange juice and tried to brace herself. No way to say it but straight out. "Mother, we have to call off the wedding."

Jim Taylor's cup clattered to the saucer and he clumsily mopped at the spill.

Alicia Taylor stared at her daughter. "What! Are you crazy? You can't cancel a wedding in two days."

"I can't marry Ben."

"Oh, for goodness' sake! Did you have a spat?" Alicia sounded relieved. "Honey, don't be upset. Things have been so hurried and hectic and you're both tense. Prenuptial jitters. That's all it is."

"We didn't have a spat. Mother, listen. I don't—"

"No. I will not listen to a word of this. Do you want to make us the laughingstock of this town?"

Judy swallowed. Her mother did not like her plans upset. She thought of the bridal gown hanging in her closet, the gifts still arriving, the elaborate arrangements. "I'm sorry," she choked. "I...I can't. I don't love Ben."

Alicia's eyes narrowed. "Then you've been putting on a good act for the past two months. Wouldn't you say so, Jim?"

Jim hesitated, cleared his throat. "I thought... Well, you did seem to hit it off right away."

"I know." Judy licked her lips. How could she explain it? It was like her head had been in the clouds since her stepfather had introduced her to Ben Cruz.

"Be nice to him," Jim had said. "He's thinking of coming into the business."

It had been easy to be nice to the handsome, free-spending young man. It seemed he was always around as both Jim and Alicia were quite taken with him. And, yes, to be honest, she had been quite taken with him herself. He was always fun and she had loved dancing with him, enjoyed his tales of exciting business deals he had pulled since his graduation from Yale. It had been romantic and flattering to have the undivided attention of such a rich, dynamic and daring entrepreneur. Perhaps, she thought now, she had been so absorbed with the image that she forgot to look at the man.

Until last night. When his kisses had become more demanding than romantic. When he had tried to...to touch her. The wave of revulsion had shocked her. A woman ought not to feel that way about the man she was going to marry.

Hard to explain. "He...he's not the right man for me."

"Ben Cruz is the right man for any woman who can catch him!" Alicia screamed. "You don't know how lucky you are because you don't know beans about men!"

This sent Judy into a sudden rage. "And who's fault is that? You kept me so caged up in that fancy girls' school that I hardly saw a boy except at the well supervised monthly dances. No wonder I fell for the first guy that gave me a tumble!"

"You've been out of that prep school for over two years. And if you'd gone to Georgetown U., where we wanted you to go, you'd have met plenty of eligible men...the right sort, too!"

"I'm not going to college to meet men."

"Oh, no! You must have a career! And just because State is tops in Architectural Design. And all your spare time at that lumberyard. You didn't need to work. You know that Jim would—"

"I know." But she didn't want to be dependent on Jim forever. Besides... "Mother, what better place to learn about the different kinds of wood? Even if I am just the bookkeeper—"

"All I'm saying is that it's not our fault that you've had no time to date as many men as you please. Believe me, missy, a good husband has a career beat all to pieces! And why you can't see that is beyond me."

Because I'm not you, was on the tip of Judy's tongue. But she didn't say it. No need to criticize her mother. But, unlike Alicia, she was determined never to be dependent on anyone. "I want to be an architect."

"All right! All right!" Alicia gave an impatient wave of her hand. "Have at it! Ben doesn't mind. That's another point in his favor. Have your little hobby. But don't miss out on this opportunity. You are lucky to have met the perfect man for you." Her voice softened and she took Judy's hand. "You know I only want you to be happy. That's why I pushed Ben... Oh, don't look at me like that. I admit it. I knew the minute I met him that he was perfect for you. Such a good-natured, engaging, charming young man. Good-looking, too, and rich! He loves you, Judy, and will take care of you."

"I can take care of myself and I won't marry a man I don't love!"

"Stop saying that. You don't mean it. You can't be in love one minute and out the next because of some crazy momentary impulse!" Alicia stood up now, her face reflecting rage as well as determination. "Besides it's too late. I will not allow you to ruin your life and make me look like a blathering idiot just because you've got a case of prenuptial jitters!"

"It's not—"

"I don't care what it is. You're not in this by yourself, missy. This wedding means as much to me and Jim as it does to you. Do you want to mess up our lives, too?"

"But..." What was her mother talking about? Judy looked at her stepfather. He looked...scared?

"Tell her, Jim," her mother prompted.

He seemed reluctant. "Oh, Alicia, this is between me and him. If Judy doesn't want—"

"Judy doesn't know what she wants. And it certainly will make a difference if she disgraces him in front of the whole town! Tell her."

"What is it, Jim?" Judy asked.

"It's just that he said he might come into the business."

"I know. You told me."

"I didn't tell you that he planned to invest two hundred and fifty thousand dollars and that...well, right now I need that kind of capital."

"Oh." Of course. That was what Ben did, invest in different businesses. He had told her. But... "It's been two months. What's holding him up? If he means to invest—"

"I don't know why the delay." Jim looked frustrated. "I thought after the wedding, when he's part of the family... But, Judy, if you don't want to—"

"Stop it I tell you! It's too late. Judy, honey, you can't make a decision like this just because of a silly moment's notion. You'll regret it the rest of your life. And it will affect all of us."

Her mother kept talking, but Judy wasn't listening. She was looking at the ashen face of the man who had been the only father she had known since she was four years old. When her mother had said, "This is your new daddy. He's going to take care of us." He had done just that. He had given her love, support, whatever she asked.

Now when he needed her....

She did like Ben. At least she had. Maybe her mother was right. Maybe it was just prenuptial jitters.

Maybe it was natural to feel apprehensive, afraid of an intimacy she had never before experienced.

Her mother. Did she really want to make her look a fool?

The wedding was all set. The reception. Only two days.

She looked again at her stepfather. He looked defeated. Helpless.

It was as if she held two hundred and fifty thousand dollars in her hand and refused to give it to him.

CHAPTER ONE

JAKE Mason took his seat in the golf cart, glanced at his watch, and swore. The ceremony was to be in Elmwood, Virginia, an hour's drive from Wilmington. "We'd better get a move on or I'll be late for the damn wedding."

"*Damn* wedding?" Scot Harding queried as he steered toward the seventeenth hole at the Overland Country Club.

"Damn *all* weddings," Jake retorted with disdain.

"Got a thing against them?"

"Right. Well...not really. It's just that they're apt to be contagious."

Scot grinned. "I see what you mean. Particularly with you being so eligible...like rich, man. And today...best man, maid of honor. You're set up, chum."

"Not me! I'll hand over the ring, toast the happy couple, and out. I made sure not to get acquainted with the maid of honor, the bride, or anybody else likely to be there. I told Ben I'd have to skip all the nuptial build-up on account of this and that...you know."

"And because you don't want to be touted as his best friend when you know damn well you're not."

11

"Oh, come on, Scot. The guy saved my life, you know."

"God, man! That was ten years ago! I think you've returned the favor."

"Can't ever return a favor like that." Jake shuddered, even now seeing the headlights of the speeding car that had jumped the curb as he was about to turn and enter the frat house. Ben Cruz, who was coming out at the same time, literally hit him with a flying tackle that moved both of them from the path of the speeding car. And from sheer death, judging by the impact of the crash as the car plowed into the building. "I would have had it if it hadn't been for Ben."

"And he'd have lost the best friend a freeloader ever had. Wasn't it you who paid off his gambling debts when the mob was after him? That guy was always into some mess."

"Yep, but it was always an interesting mess. College wouldn't have been the same without Ben." Jake smiled, remembering the quick savvy of the young hired man—never a student—who had done odd jobs about the campus and waited table at their frat house. "He was always good for a laugh."

"And you were always good for a touch. Tell me, how many times have you seen him since Yale?" Scot grabbed his club and followed Jake onto the tee.

"Well...oh, from time to time."

Scot grunted. "Every time he needed a stake. Scored twice, that I know about, didn't he? A pizza parlor and a bowling alley, both of which bombed."

"Yep." Jake gave his golf club a practice swing. "Ben's not been too successful at handling money."

"A born loser you mean."

"But a good one," Jake said. "Never lost that smile or handy excuse for the failure. Ben's always up. An engaging guy."

"All con men are." Scot shook his head. "And you let him con you. You're a pushover. Has to do with your guilt complex."

Jake's brow quirked. "Guilt complex?"

"Sure. How come all that money landed in your lap when some people don't have anything? Good thing all that Mason gold is tied up in trusts or some such knots, else you'd give it all away."

"Oh, shut up."

"Truth hurts, huh?" Scot regarded him soberly. "Well, you might as well face it. Ben Cruz is a con and you're a soft touch. So you didn't attend his bachelor party, but I bet my bottom dollar you financed it."

Jake didn't answer, just smiled as he placed his ball on the tee and scanned the horizon. He wasn't about to tell Scot what else he had financed. His wedding present, a check in the amount of two hundred and fifty thousand dollars had been delivered at the bachelor party. He had purposely delayed the gift until just before the wedding. Wanted to make sure Ben was marrying the daughter of his proposed partner, a man with thirty years' experience in construction. A wife and a good business partner ought to keep Ben on

track. A good situation for Ben this time, Jake thought
as he hit his ball straight down the fairway.

At Elmwood, Virginia, Ben Cruz echoed the same
sentiment. A pretty good deal, he thought as he de-
posited the check. He sure didn't plan to dump all
that into Taylor Construction. He'd already persuaded
Mr. Taylor to take less. The man was in a hurt. Wonder why?

Any way you look at it, it's a pretty good deal for
me. Just lay down the cash, sit back and collect the
profits while Taylor does the work. What's more, the
money was a gift. A wedding gift. You couldn't beat
that with a stick. Plus a bonus...getting hitched to a
neat number ten like Judith Taylor...five feet four and
not an ounce over a hundred and five delicate perfectly fashioned pounds. He walked out of the bank
thinking of that delicious body nestled in his arms.
That mane of honey blond hair across his chest and
those big blue eyes gazing up at him. Tonight. He got
excited just thinking about it.

Bit of a cold fish, though. He wasn't used to that
shrinking violet don't-touch-me type. Sometimes he
suspected that the Taylors had pushed her into this
match.

No, he thought. Couldn't be that. She liked him,
didn't she? Hell, she ought to. All that wining and
dining. She liked to dance, and was almost as good
as he. He knew what she liked and kept her laughing.
He always made out with the broads. He hadn't
pushed. He'd sensed that Judy was...well, sorta shy

and untouched. Tonight he'd touch her. He'd show her what was what. He could hardly wait.

He reached his car, and his mind returned to the money. He'd pay off his current gambling debt, and whittle Taylor down some more if at all possible, and have plenty in his own stash. It was four hours before the wedding. He'd swing by the office. Taylor might be there.

He parked and leaped up the back steps to the second-story office space. He saw the sign even before he reached the door. Closed By The IRS. Puzzled, he retreated and ran to the front entrance. More of the same. It read Closed By The IRS. Below it, in smaller letters: Property Of The U.S. Government.

Ben was nonplussed. Perplexed. Devastated. This was a new experience for him.

Was Taylor a drug dealer? No. He's in debt. Taxes.

Aha! This is why the partnership offer. The old S.O.B. is broke. And the government has taken over.

Man, oh, man, lucky I stopped by. What an out! All I got to do is pay off the mob and go scot-free with the rest.

Judy?

Hell, number tens are a dime a dozen. Not so cold, either, especially when you were loaded. As I am at present, thanks to good old Jake.

Jake showered and dressed at the club, leaving in good time. But the traffic was pretty heavy, and he pulled into the Elmwood church parking lot a scant half hour before the ceremony. A plump woman, a tiny plastic-covered dress in one hand while the other held on to a little girl, directed him to a side door entrance.

"I'm the flower girl," the youngster announced, smiling up at him.

"A very pretty flower girl!" he said, as he held open the door for them.

"Not yet! Not 'till I get my dress on," she called over her shoulder, as they hurried down the hall.

Smiling, he found his way to the pastor's study where he was to meet Ben.

Ben was not there.

The two men who occupied the small compactly furnished office greeted him cordially, but absently, as if thinking of something else. The Reverend Joseph Smalley sat at his desk engrossed in some text. Probably the marriage ritual, which, Jake thought, he should know by heart by now.

Mr. Taylor, the bride's father, was nervously pacing the floor and kept looking at his watch.

Where was Ben?

Evidently Taylor was thinking the same thing. For, after a few minutes, he nodded toward the minister and, receiving permission, picked up the phone. He dialed. Listened. Finally he slammed down the phone and, looking extremely perturbed, stalked out of the study.

The minister glanced at Jake. "I better see what's

happening. Be right back,'' he said, as he also hurried out.

Jake shrugged. Still fifteen minutes before the scheduled ceremony. He walked to the window and looked out at the parking lot, expecting to catch sight of a hurrying Ben among the mob of arriving guests.

In the bridal chamber, Alicia Taylor studied her reflection in the long mirror, as if to confirm the exquisite perfection of her silk turquoise formal, the still youthful beauty of her facial features under the carefully applied makeup. Satisfied, she turned to inspect her daughter, enveloped in the jewel-encrusted custom gown from Sak's bridal salon. Not the top of the line, but all they could afford, under the present circumstances. Rather, could not afford. It had been charged. But, after today, when Ben was part of the family…charged.

She smiled as she gave Judy's veil a gentle tug. "I think it should be off her face a bit more.''

"No, it's just right,'' Celia, Judy's best friend and only attendant, admonished. "Well, maybe. Just a little. What do you think, Judy? Come over here to the mirror.''

Judy stood at the mirror, and blinked at the stranger in yards of rhinestone-studded organza. A mannequin in a bridal gown.

"Hold still,'' Alicia said.

Judy tried to be still as they fussed over the veil. But she wanted to run. What was she doing here, waiting to be married to a man she wished she had never met?

"You look pretty." The child in the long pink dress looked up at her in awed admiration.

"Thank you, Dottie," Judy said, touching one of the little girl's yellow curls. "You look very pretty, too."

"Let's hope she stays that way 'till she makes it down the aisle," said the child's anxious mother. "Oh, here's the photographer, Mrs. Taylor."

"Good!" Alicia said. "Stand right here, Judy. I want him to get a picture of me arranging your veil. That's right. Now, move over here while…"

Judy moved this way and that as directed, while the photographer snapped pictures, and the cheerful chatter of the others resounded in her ears. Like a death knell.

"Smile, honey!"

She smiled, trying to banish the dreadful leaden feeling. She liked Ben, didn't she? At least until just a few nights ago. Now… Prenuptial jitters, her mother called it. That's all it was. After tonight…

Tonight. She shuddered.

"Alicia, I need to speak with you." Jim Taylor, at the door, beckoned to his wife.

"Not now, Jim. The photographer—"

"Now!"

As if impelled by the urgency in his voice, Alicia went out, closing the door behind her.

The others waited, their chatter subdued.

When Alicia returned, her face was ashen. "You!" she sputtered, staring at Judy. "How *could* you!"

"Mother, what..." Judy moved toward her, concerned. She looked ill.

"Don't touch me!" Alicia drawled in slow malicious contempt.

Judy stopped short, unprepared for the vicious onslaught. But pity overcame puzzlement. Alicia stood rigid, panting, chest heaving, as if on the verge of a stroke. "Oh, Mother, do sit down," she implored.

Alicia stepped back, then gazed wildly around as if seeing the others for the first time. "Get...!" She stopped, as if fighting desperately for control. "Please. I must speak to my daughter alone!"

They dispersed quickly, looking curious and apprehensive.

"So you did it anyway, didn't you?" Alicia shouted almost before they filed out. "In spite of what we said."

"I...did what?"

"You sent Ben away. Don't deny it!"

"I sent...? Ben? He's not here?"

Her mother shook her head. Judy's pulse quickened, vacillating between catastrophe and relief. Ecstasy. All in a nanosecond. Ben was not here. She wouldn't have to marry him!

"You did! I see it in your face. You sent him away."

"No, I didn't. I never—"

"But you'll regret it, missy. When I think of the

expense… The humiliation! Dear God, how can I face those people out there?''

Judy looked at her mother, trying to make sense of what she was saying. Ben was not here? Why? She hadn't said anything to him that…. She tried to think. Last night, at the rehearsal, he hadn't acted any different. In fact he had been in an unusually good mood. ''Mother, maybe he's just late,'' she said, a lump rising in her throat as relief faded.

''Oh, no. He's gone. You tell her, Jim,'' Alicia prompted as the door opened and Jim Taylor came in.

''He's gone, Judy,'' he confirmed.

''Gone?'' But where would Ben go? And why? ''You mean he's not here, but—''

''Not here and not coming.'' Jim looked more puzzled than angry. ''He left town, Judy. I tried to phone him and his phone was disconnected. So I went to his apartment. He's left…cleared out. The superintendent said he didn't even leave a forwarding address.''

''You needn't look so surprised, young lady. You manipulated the whole thing, didn't you?'' Alicia looked accusingly at her daughter. ''After you promised. After we wouldn't call off the wedding, you made Ben do it.''

''Mother, I never said one word to Ben to make him think—''

''Why else would he leave? If you even hinted at all that stuff you told us just two days ago. I can just hear you.'' Alicia's voice rose high in fury. '' 'I don't really love you... You're not right for me... We'd better call it off!'"

"Mother, I never. I swear I didn't," Judy choked, stung by the injustice of the accusation.

"You must have said or done something. Why else would he leave?"

Why indeed? Judy wondered. Had she unknowingly imparted how she felt? Had her prudishness turned him off? Perhaps he sensed...

"You remember now, don't you?" Alicia flung the words at her. "But you'll regret it, missy. You'll regret it the rest of your life!"

Jim put an arm around his wife. "Honey, don't blame Judy. She's here. It's Ben who—"

"Oh, no. It's her. You heard her the other day. And now..." She turned to Judy. "Do you know what you've done? You've embarrassed us before the whole town. Humiliated us! Dear Lord! How can I stand this?" Alicia collapsed into a chair, the tears streaming down her face, splattering onto the silk gown she had so happily donned a short hour before. "Oh, how could you! After all we've done for you."

"But I didn't say anything to Ben. I didn't." Judy looked at her stepfather, feeling a tremor of guilt. Could Ben have sensed what she didn't say?

Her mother was almost hysterical.

"God sent us an angel, and you sent him away! I'll never forgive you. Never! Oh, how could you!"

"Come, Alicia. No need to blame Judy. Be reasonable," Jim said.

But Alicia was beyond reason. She released all her venom on Judy, berating her as "a vicious, scheming, ungrateful wretch."

Judy, stunned into silence, could only listen, until Jim hustled Alicia out. "We'll have to face our guests, honey. Explain."

Judy watched them go. Her head pounded. Her body trembled, jolted by a riotous tumult of conflicting emotions. Shame. Exultation. Guilt.

She didn't have to marry Ben.

Guests waiting... Her mother was so embarrassed...

Had she done this?

It wasn't her fault. Or was it?

Her head ached so. Perhaps...an aspirin. She steadied herself against the mirror, and reached for her purse.

Her hand shook as she opened the bottle and lifted it to pour out a couple of tablets.

The minister came back to inform Jake that the wedding had been canceled.

"Canceled? Why?"

"The groom..." Rev. Smalley hesitated, as if not knowing how to put it. "For some reason has been...er...unable to attend."

Jake was blunt. He knew Ben. "Unable? Or unwilling?" he asked.

The embarrassed minister admitted that it seemed the groom had left town.

Jake was puzzled. What kind of scam was Ben pulling? He tried to think. Yes, he had refused Ben the money until he had checked out that there really was a Taylor Construction, and yes, he had told Ben he'd get the money when he married the daughter.

Rev. Smalley shook his head. "I don't understand. He was here last night for the wedding rehearsal. And now it seems, he has left town. No warning. Poor Judy. This is a blow. And she's such a sweet girl. In fact, the whole family... Mrs. Taylor is one of our deaconesses, you know. Such a lovely woman. And she went all out for this. Judy is her only daughter." He shook his head again. "Such a pity! I don't understand it."

Jake didn't understand it, either. The girl must be a lemon, he supposed, for Ben to back out of the marriage, and a deal that would have landed him a steady income. Probably didn't intend to marry her anyway. Just a scheme to get his hands on a few lousy bucks. Damn!

"Yes. A pity," Jake agreed, starting out.

"Wait. Don't hurry away. I'm sure..." The minister paused, as if in a quandary. "That is, everything is all set up in the social hall. All these guests... I'm sure they will go forward with the reception."

"Thank you," Jake said. But there was no need for him to stick around. He didn't know anybody, and he had no wish to gape at the jilted bride. Damn! All this preparation. The guests. He walked down the hall thinking of the little girl. "I'm the flower girl!" So proud and happy. And now...

He stopped beside an open door, shocked to see a woman in a bridal gown lift a bottle. The bride! She was going to...

"Don't!" He rushed in and knocked the bottle from her hand. "He's not worth it."

She lifted a harassed, tormented face to him. "Get me out of here! Please!"

CHAPTER TWO

JAKE hesitated, but only for a moment, anxiety overcoming discretion. A woman on the verge of suicide...

She gave him no chance to hang back. She threw the train of her gown over one arm and pulled him into the hall. Then looked uncertainly around.

"This way," he said. He could at least take her home. She was in no state to face that crowd. She followed blindly as he led her down the steps, through the parking lot to his car.

Incredibly, they encountered no one, not even in the parking lot. Probably the surprised guests, sympathetic and curious, were at the reception. And the social hall must be on the other side of the sanctuary, he thought with relief. He wouldn't like to be seen absconding with the main attraction.

He glanced at the woman. She was no lemon. In fact, quite lovely. Again he wondered about Ben. Well...maybe not his type. Not that he knew much about Ben's women, but the only ones he had seen him with were the sultry knowing kind. The woman huddled in the seat beside him, looked as innocent as a child. A child who was ashamed to be caught playing grown-up in somebody's bridal gown. He could

25

have laughed had he not felt an overwhelming pity for her.

And if he wasn't in the middle of a damn traffic jam. He glanced at the slow-moving car beside his. The woman passenger's eyes twinkled and she waved. "Congratulations!"

Damn! The bridal gown!

He returned the greeting with a sheepish grin. At least she didn't know him from Adam! As soon as he could, he turned off into a relatively quite street. "Take off that veil!"

"Oh!" The crisp demand seemed to shock her out of her apathy. She snatched the veil off, flung it to the floor, carelessly crumbling it underfoot. "I'm sorry," she said, really looking at him for the first time. "We must appear—"

"A happy just-married couple." He smiled, hoping to ease the tension.

"Yes." She did not return the smile. "Oh, it was awful of me to grab you like I did. I just wanted to get out of there, and you came in..." Her gaze sharpened, taking in his formal attire. "You were to be in the wedding! You're Ben's best friend? Joe...no, Jake. Jake..."

"Jake Mason," he supplied, flinching as he remembered Scot's words that morning. "Being touted as his best friend when you know damn well you're not."

"You were going to be best man."

He nodded.

"Do you know what happened? Where Ben is? Why…?" she stopped, suddenly aware of his puzzled discomfort. "I'm sorry. Of course you don't know," she said, realizing that he had been waiting at the church, just as she had been. "I am sorry to have imposed on you."

"No problem." He bent toward her. "Are…are you all right?"

She heard the anxiety in his voice and flushed. He was pitying her, just as Celia and all her friends back at the church were pitying her. While she… She couldn't help it. She was glad! Glad that Ben hadn't shown up. The suffocating coil that bound her had suddenly snapped, and she could breathe. She wanted to dance and sing and shout with—

"Shall I take you home?"

"No!" She swallowed, hoping she hadn't screamed. But she wasn't ready to face her mother and all her recriminations. Not yet. She swallowed again. "I don't want to go home."

"Where then?" He had parked on a side street bordering the park and now his whole attention was on her, his expression still anxious.

She stared at him, hearing shouts at a baseball game a short distance away. She tried to think. She could go to Celia's. But that would be the first place they'd look. She looked down. "My purse! I left it at the church."

"Shall I go back? I could—"

"No." The last place she wanted to be.

"They…my mother will get it. I was just…I was thinking I could go to a hotel, but I don't have—"

"Money's not the problem." He caught her blank look and added, "You'd be rather conspicuous in that garb."

"Oh. Well, I guess…if you could drop me at home," she said. But she looked as bewildered and defenseless as a kitten about to be drowned.

He couldn't stand it. "We could go down to my boat."

"Your…? You have a boat and we could… You wouldn't mind?" Her words tumbled eagerly over each other. "It would give me chance to…to think. Would it be all right?"

"Sure. We're not dressed for a sail, but what the hell!" he said as he switched on the engine.

"Wait!" She turned her back to him and pointed. "This thing hooks on. If you'd unfasten it…" He obliged, and she rolled the train into a bundle, picked up the veil, and got out of the car. A couple of women at a family picnic watched in wonder as she dumped the costly finery into a convenient waste container.

He also watched in wonder. She didn't look like a heartbroken reject on the verge of suicide now. She didn't look like a drowning kitten, either. She was a woman in charge, saying "Get the hell out of my way!"

Her mood changed, however, during the long, mostly silent, drive to Delaware. By the time they reached the dock the lost look was back, accompanied by a question... "Where do I go from here?"

He had put that look there, or at least helped get her into this predicament. It cut him to the quick. It hadn't much mattered that Ben had conned him time and time again. But he had allowed him to con this innocent young...

"How old are you?" he asked, as he pulled into his parking slot at the yacht club.

"Twenty-three next month."

A mere kid, he thought, as he led her across the almost deserted dock.

Judy was in a daze, still trying to grapple with what had happened, trying to face the consequences. But even her befuddled mind alerted at sight of the boat. Not a small sailboat, but... Of course! This was Ben's friend, his classmate at Yale. Ben had helped him on many deals. He must be as rich as Ben, she thought as she followed down a small flight of steps, through a companionway to...an honest-to-goodness bedroom! Small, but giving an illusion of luxury and space that boggled her decorator's mind.

He walked through an adjoining door, and she heard him open and shut what sounded like a cabinet door. "I think you'll find everything you need," he said when he returned. "Would you like something to eat...or to drink?"

She shook her head, wishing he would go away. All she wanted was to bury her face in one of those pillows and blank out today...tomorrow...everything.

"All right." He looked uncertain. "Well, if you need anything. Oh!" He opened a drawer of the built-in cabinet. "I thought so. Mel left some things. If you want to change…" He made a help-yourself gesture.

"Thank you."

He gave her another uncertain look, then started out. Turned back, nodded toward the bedside phone. "Maybe you'd better call your parents."

She shook her head.

"You don't have to say where you are. Just let them know you're okay."

"All right." But she didn't move from where she was standing.

"You wouldn't want them to be worried. Maybe send out an all points bulletin." He waited, like he wasn't going anywhere until she phoned.

She sat on the bed, forced herself to pick up the phone. Dialed. "Mother, I'm—"

"Judy! Where are you?" Alicia sounded both agitated and angry.

"I'm all right."

"Where *are* you?"

"On…at a friend's."

"Who? Where? Jim will come and get you."

"No." She looked up at the man still standing in the doorway. "I'd like to stay here awhile."

"Judy! We need to thrash this out! See if we can find Ben and—"

"I'll call you. Goodbye, Mother." She put down

the phone, turned again toward the door. The door was shut. He was gone.

She stretched across the bed. If she could just rest for a minute. Think.

When he tapped at the door an hour later, there was no answer. He opened the door as quietly as he could, and stepped inside. She lay motionless on the bed, and he stood for a moment looking down at her.

The golden rays of the setting sun drifted through the porthole, spotlighting a beautiful picture. She still wore her wedding dress and the jewels in its lustrous folds sparkled like stars. Her hair, released from the confining veil, cascaded over the pillow, a heavy mass of gold. But it was the face that held him. A pretty face in its heart-shaped perfection, the small tilted nose, the long lashes fringing the closed eyelids. But Jake Mason, accustomed to pretty faces, was struck by something else. She looked so young and innocent. So vulnerable.

He was glad to see her sleeping. A deep sleep. Not induced by drugs, for he had checked the bathroom to make sure of that. No, this was the sleep of pure exhaustion. Induced by hectic prenuptial preparations, excitement…shock. His fists clenched. He could throttle Ben!

Then, surprisingly, he smiled. She had escaped. She didn't know it, but she was better off without Ben. She'd get over this. He took off her slippers, covered her with a blanket, and left as quietly as he had come.

*   *   *

When Judy awoke, the bright rays of an early sunrise were streaming into the room. For a moment she stared up at the ceiling, wondering why it sloped instead of... She sat bolt upright. Looked down at her crumpled gown. Looked around.

Remembered.

The first sensation was one of overwhelming relief. She was not married to Ben. She wouldn't have to marry him.

Unless... A wary chill crept along her spine.

No. She wouldn't marry him even if he did come back.

He wouldn't. Jim had said... "Cleared out... No forwarding address."

Mother! Pale and angry, her lips curling with scorn. "God sent an angel... You sent him away!"

Judy felt a flash of anger. I didn't send him away! And Ben's no angel! He's just a man.

A chuckle erupted in her throat. Another. Mother's angels always came in the shape of a man... "Jim, your new daddy...an angel come to take care of us." "Ben...an angel..." The thought of Ben as an angel was so funny. The series of chuckles dissolved into a fit of hysterical laughter. Judy gave way to it. She lay back on the bed and laughed and laughed, her head rocking from side to side, tears streaming down her cheeks. She couldn't stop. Laughter burst from her like an out-of-control flood, somehow releasing the anger, frustration, guilt...all that was bottled inside her.

She felt the weight lift, the laughter subside. She was free.

She sat up. Refreshed. Alert.

She was on a boat. This friend of Ben's, Jake somebody, had been so kind. He had brought her here. She had lain down for a minute and had fallen asleep.

She got up and began to fold the blanket, looking around as she did so. Some boat! This one room…so beautiful, so spacious! Actually, not so spacious, she thought, surveying it again with an architect's critical eye. Smooth, compact lines. The color also contributed to the feeling of space. A pale blue that made it one with outside sea and sky. The same blue color covered everything, walls, spread, carpet…a monotonous tone that also created a sense of space. She surveyed the sloping ceiling, the compact built-in wall cabinets that took not one inch of space from the little room. Oh, it had been so cleverly, so beautifully done!

Judy moved around the room, touching the light wood, feeling the texture, taking in the effect of the monotonous pale blue color. The sight of a well-designed room always stimulated and inspired her. She could do this! She was full of ideas just waiting to be transformed into homes of inviting comfort and beauty. The thought excited and vitalized her. She wanted to be up and doing.

But not in this cumbersome fancy gown, for goodness' sake! She remembered now that he had told her to help herself, that Mel always left something.

She opened a drawer, wondering. Who was Mel? His girlfriend or maybe his wife. Where was she?

And where was he? Had he gone home and left her alone on this boat?

No. Or, if so, he'd be back, she thought, instinctively believing he would not leave her stranded.

She was right. By the time she had showered in the little bathroom and changed into the pale blue shorts and shirt, which almost fit and would do for now, she heard his knock on the door. She opened it.

"Good morning. You're...all right?" As if to cover his obvious surprise, he quickly added, "I mean...you found everything you need?"

"Yes, thank you." She touched the shorts and looked up at him. "Are you sure it's all right?" she asked, remembering the Armani label.

"Sure I'm sure. Mel probably forgot she left them."

Not likely, she thought. Pale blue like the room. Probably Mel, whoever she is, leaves the proper matching attire at every place she inhabits. The thought evoked another gurgle of laughter which she managed to suppress.

"Are you hungry?"

"Oh, yes!" Starving, now that the weight had lifted. She felt so good!

He was almost disconcerted by that smile. The way one corner of her mouth lifted, the radiance of those wide blue eyes. Clearly, she was not one to burden others with her distress. He liked that. "This way, madame." He gave a servile nod as he held open the door.

"This is absolutely the most delightful smell in the entire world," she said, wrinkling her nose as she was seated at the little table in the galley.

"Oh?"

"Coffee brewing and bacon frying. Don't you just love it?"

"Yes. Butter that toast," he said, hearing the slices pop up. He took the bacon out of the microwave, poured the eggs over the melting cheese.

"And it's so lovely." She obediently buttered the toast, but her eyes scanned the U-shaped booth with soft leather cushions, the tiny but efficient cooking area with the blue tile counters. "Who did it?"

"Did it?"

"The boat. Who was the architect...the decorator?"

He shrugged. "I've no idea. Why? Are you interested in boats?"

"Not boats exactly. But structure and design."

"I see." He set plates of bacon and eggs on the table, reached for the coffeepot.

She began to eat with relish, as if she didn't have a care in the world. "Oh, this is so good and I'm so hungry!"

Like yesterday never happened. Well, he wouldn't mention it, either. "So you like my boat?"

"Oh, yes. It's so beautifully put together. The materials so perfect...the light balsam wood and the simplicity of fixtures." She kept talking about details he had never considered. "The smooth built-ins. The illusion of space created by that pale blue color throughout."

"Yeah. That's why I call her the *Bluebird*," he said.

"Of course! Boats have names, don't they? The *Bluebird*." She closed her eyes as if considering. "Perfect. Did you request that color?"

"Nope. I requested nothing. Ran across it at a boat show last year, liked it, bought it. As is."

"Oh. Just like…that." She paused, and the mischievous twinkle in her eyes made him wonder what she had started to say and didn't. "I can see why you like it," she said after a moment. "Can you sail it? By yourself, I mean. It's so big."

"It's not so big." Certainly not as large as his yacht, he thought. "Of course I can manage her alone. Would you like to go for a sail?"

"Oh, yes! Could we? I've never sailed before, not even in a little boat. But this…oh, that would be wonderful!"

He watched her, enchanted by the smile that lifted the corner of her mouth and lit her face with a glow of pure delight. She looked like an excited child anticipating a marvelous adventure.

Then, as swiftly as it had come, the smile faded. The eyes narrowed, the glow dimmed, eclipsed by the shadow of yesterday. Yesterday. She had hid it so well. She had almost made him forget the distraught woman about to swallow a bottle of pills. The memory pained him. "I'd better not," she said.

"Why not?" He was sorry that the glow had gone. Angry with Ben.

"I have to...to go home," she said, sternly reminding herself that she had to face it. Her mother's wrath, Jim's disappointment. Evidently he had really been counting on Ben's investment.

"Why?"

She looked up, startled that he sounded so belligerent. "There are things I have to do," she explained. Details. Return gifts with a little explanatory note. Embarrassing to say you were dumped and didn't know why. What *would* she say? Incompatibility? No, that was for divorces, wasn't it. Also she needed to call Casey, her boss, ask for her job back. That was going to be awkward, too, after that going-away party they had held for her in the employees' cafeteria. Well, she'd just have to—

"Things can wait, can't they!" The question and the noisy clatter of the dishes he was stacking broke into her musing.

"Oh, I'm sorry," she said, getting up to help clear the table. "I've been sitting here dreaming while you work. Where do I put the butter?" He nodded toward a built-in fridge that looked like one of the cabinets. Neat.

"Well, can't they?" he asked as he carelessly loaded the dishwasher.

"What?"

"Things…whatever you have to do. They'll be there whenever you get there, won't they? After all, you weren't scheduled for a quick return. Weren't you supposed to be away on your honeymoon or… God! I'm sorry."

"Oh, you mustn't be!" she said, touched by his consternation. He was apologizing for reminding her of yesterday's fiasco, a subject they had been skirting all morning. He, out of pity for her while she… "It's all right. I…" She stopped. To say she was overjoyed at being dumped would make her look more a fool than she already was. "I'll survive," she finished. "And you're right. I wouldn't be at home if…if things were different. If you don't mind, I'd love to go for a sail. One more day away wouldn't matter, would it?"

As many days as it will take, he thought, to keep that smile on her face.

CHAPTER THREE

JUDY followed Jake up a ladder, and stood beside him on what he called the "flying bridge." From this high focal point, she watched as he steered the *Bluebird* from the wharf. Others were also sailing out or boarding their craft to fix, polish, or just sit and picnic. Everyone, including Jake, seemed to know everyone else and festive greetings and jokes flew from boat to boat. Two children, enveloped in safety gear, looked up and waved to Judy, involving her in the revelry.

She returned their greeting, laughter again bubbling within her. She was having a holiday. She was not, as had been planned for two months, on a honeymoon with Ben. Instead, she was going for a sail with a man who was practically a stranger, and she felt happier than she had felt in a long time.

Why was she so happy? The man beside her?

Goodness, she hardly knew him. Yesterday, she had latched onto him because he was there. A bulwark against what had happened. An escape from curiosity, recriminations, embarrassment. She had hardly looked at him. She had just grabbed and held on. Shamelessly!

What must he think of her? Heat flooded her face. She forced herself to look at him—possibly for the first time. Yesterday was a blur. Even earlier this morning she had been more interested in his boat than him.

He was quite handsome. Thick unruly sun-bleached hair so striking against deeply sun-bronzed skin. Clearly a man who spent a lot of time outdoors. Regular features, full lips, keen nose, slightly tilted, contributing to that expression of…arrogance? No, she decided. Just pleasantly aloof, as if he didn't care what you thought of him. Just like he didn't care that the pullover he was wearing was faded, and the jeans that hugged his long lean legs bore oil stains. He wore them with the same casual elegance that he had worn yesterday's tux. He stood on bare feet, strong fingers gripping the steering gear. Eyes as clear and blue as the sky above squinting in alert attention. He was concentrating on getting the *Bluebird* safely past the surrounding craft, and out to sea.

It occurred to her that this was his way. Full concentration on the present moment.

Yesterday she had said, "Get me out of here," and he had done just that. No whys or wherefores, no probing.

This morning, he had been intent upon her momentary needs…clothes, food. He had supplied both. Still no probing.

Even entertainment, just as if she had been an invited guest. "Would you like to go for a sail? Things can wait." As good as saying, *Forget yesterday and tomorrow. Enjoy today.*

"Well, Judy Taylor, you couldn't have picked a better day."

His attention now centered on her and a warm glow stole through her. "A better day?"

"For a first sail."

"Oh?" She looked around and realized they were now out of the harbor and cruising through the water at a rather rapid rate of speed.

"Wind, weather, and water...perfect day," he said.

"Yes," she agreed, loving the warmth of the sun on her back, the wind whipping through her hair, the sensation of whizzing through space. She was silent for a long time, absorbing the feeling.

"Like it?" he asked.

"Love it." Loved standing beside him, bare feet bracing the floorboards as the boat skimmed the surface of the water. She felt a wonderful sense of freedom she had never before experienced. She was vaguely aware of the few other boats they passed, the coastline some distance away with buildings and houses where people worked, played...loved and quarreled. But it had nothing to do with her. She was here. Apart. All she had to do was stand on this flying bridge and fly! She felt free as a bird. "Now I know why you call her the *Bluebird*," she said with sudden inspiration.

"You said that this morning."

"That's right! I did, didn't I? But that was different. A design thing...the blue decor. Funny," she

said, wrinkling her nose. "Blue is one of my unfa-
vorite colors."

"Oh? Should I change it?"

"No! It's perfect. I thought this morning, it brings
the outside in...the sky and the sea."

"Well, that's a relief." He sounded serious, but
there was laughter in his eyes. Blue eyes. She was
beginning to like that color.

"Anyway, now I know why you call her the *Bluebird*."

"Oh?"

She gestured with one hand, explaining. "You feel
like you're flying."

"Now that's a sensation I've always associated
with airplanes."

"No! Being in an airplane is more like being shut
up in a floating closet." She saw his lips twitch and
sniffed. "All right. Grin. But don't tell me that riding
in a plane ever made you feel like you had wings and
could fly to...to wherever!"

"That's how you feel?"

She nodded, and now the laughter bubbled up and
spilled over. "Crazy, isn't it? But that's how I feel.
Free as a bird that's just been let out of her cage."

"Oh?" He looked bewildered, as if he was trying
to figure her out.

For some reason, she felt the need to reassure him.
"It's a marvelous feeling. Really. Like I could go
anywhere, do anything I want. Just spread my wings
and take off. The sky's the limit."

"Well, that's great." I guess, he thought, staring at her. She looked excited, and...yes, happy. He wondered if it was for real.

Yesterday was for real. He had seen the pills, sensed her misery and bewilderment when she had latched onto him, a perfect stranger. And now, here she was ignoring the whole episode. Dumping it out of her mind just like she dumped that finery in the park. That wasn't healthy, was it? Should he remind her? Or help keep up the facade?

"Hey, how'd you like to go for a swim?" he asked, while he was trying to decide.

Her eyes flashed to the water below. "In that!" She made a face. "Thank you very much. But I'm feeling like a bird, not a fish."

"Well, I didn't want you to take off in space. I was just trying to bring you down to earth." He stopped, giving her a sheepish grin, because that was exactly what he had been trying to do. If she'd just give him an opener, he'd tell her Ben had done her a favor by copping out. "Anyway, I wasn't going to take you swimming in that."

"No?"

"No. There's a little beach a few miles down the coast. It's almost unaccessible from the highway, so it's usually pretty private."

"Oh, that would be fun! But..." She looked down at herself.

"I'm sure there's plenty of swimming gear. Just check." He watched her scramble down the ladder.

She sure didn't look despondent today. Why should he bring up yesterday?

Not you, buddy, you're a stranger. Remember?

Right. Leave the heart-to-heart talks to Mother or some dear and trusted friend.

Today is her day to get away from it all. You can help her fly. You're an expert at the R and R routine, aren't you?

Right!

Maybe it was the man, she thought. Maybe that was why she felt so happy.

Maybe happy wasn't the right word.

Comfortable. That was it. She had never felt so comfortable with anyone in her whole life. Anywhere. Closed in a car with him after that disastrous non-wedding or breakfasting in the boat's tiny galley, standing beside him on the bridge.

As he had predicted, she found plenty of swimsuits. All skimpy, and she had felt self-conscious when she stood before the mirror in the blue and yellow bikini she finally selected. Strangely enough, she did not feel self-conscious when she joined him. She felt right and natural, pleased to see his eyes light with admiration. She had been surprised by a stab of purely erotic pleasure at the sight of him in a skimpy pair of trunks almost the same color as his tan skin. Strange. She had seen many a man in swimming trunks and had never before been so affected. But something about him…bare chest, long lean muscular legs, and…

Oh, never mind that. Comfortable was the word. He was so quick and direct about whatever he was doing. He had anchored the boat, released the dinghy and rowed to this beautiful deserted beach, and magically produced cold drinks and blankets after they got there. Whatever she wanted to do was all right with him. He joined her as she frolicked in the water, built sandcastles, or just lay basking in the sun as she was now. Accepting her silence. No questions.

Maybe it wasn't the man. Maybe it was being away from the situation. Not striving to please her mother, or rebel against her as she had when she took the job at the lumberyard. Not trying to love Ben. She had come so close to marrying him. No obligation now. Maybe it was the release that made her so happy.

She sat up. It wasn't over yet. She had to go back. Notes. Return gifts. Face her mother... A sense of desolation swept over her. She tried to brush it off. Stood up.

Jake watched her as she began slowly to stride along the beach, kicking at the sand. It was coming back to her now. He saw the misery in her face, and felt helpless against it.

When she returned to him, however, her face was radiant. "I've been beach-combing. And look what I found." She cupped her hand, holding it like a precious jewel, for his perusal. "Isn't it beautiful?"

"Perfect." It was only a seashell. But it was lovely, its ridges curving into a perfect crescent, the delicate buff color with an almost transparent blush of pink.

"It's a symbol," she said.

"A symbol?"

"That this day is a beginning, not an end to..." She paused before concluding, "To something wonderful!"

"Right." He was glad to see the smile back. "And the day hasn't ended yet. Lunchtime! How would you fancy fresh crab?"

"Sounds great," she said, and helped him load things into the dinghy.

They caught the crab with nets lowered from the *Bluebird* and popped them into the tub of water boiling on the deck's giant hot plate. A few minutes later, they cracked the shells and feasted on the sweet crab meat. Messily. Her mother would never have tolerated such mess.

But cleaning up was easy. They simply tossed the shells overboard, and scrubbed the deck, thoroughly hosing it and themselves as they did so. It was fun.

It was almost midnight when they docked at the yacht club. The end of the happiest day she had spent in her whole life. She tried to tell him so. "It was...wonderful!"

"Then let's top it off with a nightcap," he said. "Stay put. I'll be back in a sec."

She watched him disappear into the cabin, and leaned against the rail, absorbing the peace. The lights from the clubhouse and a few surrounding boats were dimmed by the mist, and seemed as distant as the stars twinkling above. The darkness closed around her like a protective blanket, the waters lapped in rhythm against the boat, rocking it gently, lulling her into a state of utter serenity.

"Here we are." Jake returned and set a tray with the brandy and two snifters on a small table between two lounge chairs. "You make the toast." He poured and handed one glass to her.

She sat on the lounge chair, cupping the snifter, trying to say something equal to what she felt. "Isn't there a song that goes... 'When you come to the end of a perfect day and you sit alone with your thoughts'?"

"I resent that. You are not alone."

"Not exactly, but..." she bit her lip. Unflattering to say it was like being alone...being with him. Only that wasn't at all what she meant. His being there made it better. Like wearing an old shoe so comfortable you hardly knew it was on. Goodness, that wasn't what she meant, either! "What I meant...well, being with someone you really like is almost like being alone, isn't it?"

His lips twitched. "Thank you...I think."

"Oh! What I meant was that you made the day perfect. If you hadn't—"

"Never mind all that. I'm ready for my brandy. Just make the toast."

She wished she could say something momentous. Wished she could remember how the song ended. "Guess I'll have to settle for 'to the end of a perfect day.'" She lifted her glass.

"Here, here!" he said, and their glasses clicked.

She wasn't accustomed to liquor, and she took a deep breath as the liquid spread a warm glow inside her. "That's not adequate. You couldn't know what today meant to me. It gave me such a boost."

"A boost?"

She smiled. "More like a kick in the pants, I guess. I'm almost ready to go back and pick up the pieces."

"Almost?"

She flinched. Took another sip of the fiery liquid. "It's not always easy to…to face things."

"Do you want to talk about…" He hesitated. "About what happened?"

"No!" She couldn't stand his obvious sympathy. And she didn't want to talk about yesterday. "I just want to deal with tomorrow."

"Do you need more time?"

"What?"

"To be kicked or boosted, or whatever. We could sail again tomorrow."

"Tomorrow's Monday. Don't you have to go to work?"

"Work?" He looked surprised.

She grimaced. Foolish question. He probably didn't work. Just did whatever rich people did. Ben didn't work, and he was probably richer than Ben. The boat… "Saw it at a boat show. Liked it. Bought it." Just like she would buy a pair of shoes. "I meant…well, wouldn't you be busy or…or something?"

"Not tomorrow. Got a golf thing the next day and a meeting in Detroit on Thursday, but the rest of the week is clear, far as I know. Anyway, the boat is yours. For the whole week if you want it."

"But..." She stared at him, stunned by the invitation. Pleased. To relax on this boat for a whole week. Away from everything and everybody. "Do you...I mean, this isn't where you live?"

"Oh, no. I only come down when I take her out for a sail. But you would be perfectly safe. The dock is secure, and Sims, my skipper, lives only a couple of blocks away. He checks on the *Bluebird* every day, keeps everything shipshape. I'll tell him you're here and he'll look after you."

CHAPTER FOUR

SHE was glad she stayed. It was a wonderful week. They sailed again on Monday, this time in a different direction, docked at a small fishing village, at a dinky little café called The Fisherman.

"This is Judy Taylor, Abe. Abe Smoley, Judy, the owner of this famous establishment," Jake said, greeting the chubby man in shirtsleeves with the same easy familiarity with which he greeted his fellow yacht club members. "Abe, I want you to prove to her that you serve the tastiest fresh trout this side of the Atlantic, not to mention Nancy's blackberry cobbler."

"The cobbler's almost gone," said the lanky teenage waiter who turned out to be Abe's son. "But don't worry none. I'll dish yours up now."

"Thanks, Link. I knew you'd look after me," Jake said.

Link did look after them, anticipating their every need, to the disgruntlement of one of the other customers, a bearded man in a sleeveless pullover and rubber boots. "Can't see nobody else, can you, once his royal highness drops in!"

Jake laughed. "Pay him no mind, Link. He's still sore over that last little contest at which he did not shine."

"Lucky streak," the man grumbled.

"I'll show you about luck," Jake answered. "As soon as I finish this last piece of pie."

It was a tasty meal, and she enjoyed every morsel, as much as she enjoyed the gibes and sometimes crude jokes of the other diners. Here, too, everybody seemed to know everybody else. After the meal, Jake and the bearded man set up a checkerboard, and everybody in the place gathered 'round to watch the rapid-fire match. Checkers and quarters flew back and forth so fast that Judy couldn't really tell what was happening, but she gathered that Jake won from the joshing that went on as the booted one stalked out, grimly promising, "Next time!"

After the lunchtime crowd departed, Jake nodded to Link. "Come on down to the boat. I brought you something."

The "something" made Link's eyes and mouth fly open. "Gosh damn! Oh, 'scuse me, miss." He glanced at Judy. "But these are Nikes. And...they fit," he declared as he pulled one on, then the other.

"Well, you did tell me the size," Jake said.

"Yeah. Man. Bad!" Link stamped around, admiring himself.

"Well, let's go try them out," Jake said as he produced a basketball.

"Man! A good ball, too?" Link choked. "Gee, thanks, Jake."

Judy was hard put to keep up as they trotted back to the café, bouncing the ball between them. They retreated to a spot behind the detached garage, upon which hung a basketball hoop. The ground was bare and hard, as if it had been pounded by many hours of practice into a perfect playing area. She sat on an upside down tin tub and watched the contest as Jake played just as hard with the boy as he had played checkers with the bearded man. Actually Jake was pretty good.

Not as good as Link, though, who really showed off. Shooting from a distance, or turning his back to casually toss it over his shoulder…right through the hoop!

Judy was impressed. "That's great, Link! You're really good."

He grinned, brushing back his stringy blond hair, and agreed. "Yeah, I'm gonna make varsity this year. Didn't last year on account of algebra."

"Algebra?"

"Flunked. But I made it up. Jake helped me. And this year…coach says he's gonna make me starter."

"Well, you gonna stand there bragging or you gonna play?" Jake shouted.

"Okay. Okay," said the boy. "Shoot!"

Judy sat on the tub, watching the play, thinking about Jake. "Jake helped me." How did he know the boy needed help? How did he get to know these people anyway?

Maybe it wasn't such a big deal, being comfortable with Jake. Everybody was comfortable with him. She wondered why the thought depressed her.

They returned early in the evening, and Jake took off soon after. First, he introduced her to Sims, a short muscular youngish man who looked hard as nails. "He'll check in every morning and every evening. Here's his phone number. If you need anything, just call him," he said, as he was leaving. He pointed to the left. "There's a little shopping center just past the park, if you feel like browsing. See you in a day or so." He handed her an envelope, and leaped to the dock.

She watched him stride away, feeling very much alone. Abandoned.

She tried to recapture what she had felt on the bridge. That wonderful sense of freedom and power. She could go anywhere, do anything.

Not now. She felt more like a bird with a broken wing, lying helpless on the deck.

She stamped her foot, tossed her head. Judy Taylor, you are one silly gal, she told herself. Just because a man you just met has gone off about his own business...

Good heavens! Was she, like her mother, dependent upon some angel in the shape of a man to rescue her during her crisis?

No indeed. She could darn well take care of herself.

Not that she wasn't grateful. Jake Mason had given her a two day breather. Time to relax, enjoy, and think. He had given her more time, on this wonderful comfortable boat where she could sit quietly undisturbed, and make plans. Thank you, Jake Mason, she muttered, holding his envelope to her cheek.

The envelope. She opened it.

It contained three one hundred dollar bills.

He had remembered that she had come with no money and nothing but a wedding dress on her back. He had known how she felt about Mel's clothes, which didn't quite fit, and were...well, not hers. He had even told her where she could shop. No awkward offering. He had just quietly handed what he knew she needed, no questions asked.

Just as he had given Link what he so much wanted.

She liked Jake Mason.

Oh, she would pay him back of course. She still had, maybe five hundred, in her bank account. But he had given her more than money. The money, the fact that he remembered, was just the incentive she needed...to get going on tomorrow. She sat down immediately and made a list of things she must do.

The wonderful feeling was back. She was not married to Ben. She was free to fly. She knew she could get her job back, and she still had time to register for the fall term. She didn't even have to live at home anymore. Lois, the decorator Casey's secretary, was looking for someone to share her apartment. She liked Lois.

She walked around the boat, examining every aspect. It was truly a beautiful, well-designed little craft. If she could design houses as well... A profusion of colors and designs swirled through her head as she climbed into bed, but as she drifted off to sleep, one color dominated and held...the deep sea blue of a pair of eyes that squinted in the sun.

Immediately after the board meeting in Detroit, he left by plane. Upon landing in Wilmington, he went directly to the boat, surprised at how anxious he was to see her. He would have skipped the Detroit meeting, had it not been for Carl. He had met Carl Shepherd, an out-of-work electrical engineer—a victim of corporate downsizing—at the PGA Masters golf tournament in Georgia, and had been intrigued by his ideas on electrical-powered motorcars. The coming thing and we ought to be in front, Jake had thought.

He didn't know how much he had accomplished. He had no hand in running the business of Mode Motors, and was ex-officio on the board, as he was on several subsidiaries of Mason Enterprises...privileged but not exactly active. Well, it was up to Carl. He had managed to get him hired and in a strategic position. He'd have to put across his own ideas.

Jake sighed. Sometimes he felt like he was always on the outside, looking in while someone else did the work or put across an idea.

His mood brightened when he reached the club's parking lot. He was really looking forward to seeing Judy Taylor. He liked her, her enthusiasm, her musical laughter. Not diminished by what had happened. She's a spunky kid, he thought, as he loosened his tie and got out of the car. He flung his coat over his shoulder and walked toward the dock.

She was waiting for him, and waved as he approached. It was good to have someone waiting for him.

Good to have *Judy* waiting for him.

"Well, how did things go?" he asked as he stepped aboard.

"Splendidly! Just splendidly, thanks to you." He liked the way her eyes danced. Blue eyes.

"I'm glad you enjoyed the boat."

"Not just the boat. The money."

"Oh?"

"It…well, I don't know how to explain it. But I was really down in the dumps when you left. But then I opened the envelope and…wow! It was like finding a gold mine."

He grinned. "Not exactly a gold mine."

"It was to me. Like you told me to get busy and gave me the means to do it. Thank you."

"You're quite welcome. So you got busy?"

"I sure did. First I went shopping. Kinda ritzy center, but I didn't need much. Couple of shorts and tops. You like this?" she asked, turning for his inspection.

"Very much." The way those short-shorts hugged her bottom. She really had a nice figure. And that loose knit top. Yellow. Maybe that's what brought out the colour of her eyes.

"Are you hungry?" she asked, as if she were hostess. "There's sandwich stuff. And coffee."

"I ate on the plane, but I guess I could use a snack," he said and followed her down to the galley.

"And I bought stationery," she said as she pulled things from the fridge.

"Stationery?"

"Well, I sure couldn't use the embossed 'Mr. and Mrs. Benjamin Cruz' notepaper, which I had bought to send thank-you notes, could I?"

"No. Guess not," he said, wondering that she could chuckle about it, seeming perfectly at ease. At ease in his galley, too, assembling sandwiches and making fresh coffee. That pleased him.

"Anyway, that paper is at home along with the list of gifts received, which I sure could use," she said as she set plates and a platter of sandwiches on the table. "I'll have to address and attach them to the gifts to be returned when I get home. I tried to remember the people, and what gift they sent. There'll be more, of course." She sighed. "So many. But at least I got started. See, I wrote all those." She gestured to a stack of envelopes on the shelf.

"All those?"

"Oh, sure. It was easy, once I figured out what to say."

"What did...?" He broke off, wanting to kick himself. It must have been embarrassing, explaining to people who had seen her dumped at the altar.

"What did I say? Oh, just that I was returning the beautiful whatnot or your thoughtful gift, if I couldn't remember what it was."

"Your mother could have supplied that information, couldn't she?"

"Oh!" The question seemed to startle her. "Well, I guess I didn't think...didn't want to bother her." Strange, he thought as she spoke rapidly as if to divert him. "I said I was sorry our plans were so abruptly canceled. Appreciate your thoughtfulness, regret the inconvenience...that kind of thing." She poured their coffee, and joined him at the table, seemingly as unperturbed as if she had been talking of a minor unpleasantness that happened to someone else. "I'm hungry, whether you are or not," she said pointedly.

"Oh, I'll have one," he said, reaching for a sandwich. He was trying to figure her out. Was she as unaffected as she seemed? And what was it with her mother?

"I've been hungry ever since I got on this boat. I think it must be the sea air." She popped a couple of potato chips into her mouth. "Oh, yes, I phoned and got my old job back. And I talked with Lois, a woman who works at the lumberyard. I'm going to share her apartment. It's closer to work."

"That's good." He hesitated. "Did you phone your mother?" Whatever was going on between them, her mother ought to know where she was. She was not quite a minor, but all the same...

She shook her head. "But it's all right!" she exclaimed, as if reading his thoughts. "I wrote her...special delivery."

"Why didn't you phone? She must be upset."

"That's why!" She flushed, looking a little guilty. "She gets so...so excited. And...well, when she gets like that, there's no talking to her and..." She paused and looked earnestly at him. "I wrote and explained that I needed a little space...time to get over the trauma. And that wasn't a lie. It wasn't!" Was she trying to convince him or herself? "This has been very traumatic for me, can't you see that?"

"Well, yes." At least she was looking very distraught at the moment. What was it with this girl?

"And that's what I told Mother," she said, looking extremely wary.

"Will she understand?"

"She ought to! She's always going through some kind of trauma herself." It was the first time he had heard her sound bitter.

Time to change the subject. "So you'll be leaving Saturday? One more day on the *Bluebird*. What would you like to do?"

"What we did that first day," she said without hesitation. "Could we sail back to that beach and just...just do nothing?"

"We'll see. The weather's iffy."

It was another perfect day. They sailed to the same cove, anchored, and rowed in the skiff to that island she was beginning to regard as theirs. They swam a little, riding the waves which seemed higher than usual, and lolled in the sun just as they had on Monday.

"It is so pleasant here," Judy said. When there was no answer, she looked to find that Jake was lying on his stomach fast asleep. He must be tired, she thought. A day of golf, then he flew to Detroit for some kind of meeting, and straight back here, boating and swimming just because I wanted to. He has been so good to me, and he hardly knows me.

Good *for* me. What would I have done if he hadn't happened along? Like one of those angels Mother is always talking about.

Stop it, Judy Taylor! You are in charge of your own life. Not some man, angel or not.

Jake is just nice. Certainly not *your* personal angel. He has made no personal overtures. He has not touched you. Not once. He's just…nice!"

So don't go getting ideas, missy! That sounded so much like her mother that she chuckled. Still, it was good advice. After today, it was quite possible that she would never see him again.

"I wish I could stay here forever," she said, unaware that she spoke aloud until Jake answered.

"Uh-huh. Not today."

She looked up from her sand castle to see that he was awake and his eyes were focused on a dark cloud looming in the distance. "I know I should have been listening to the weather reports and not you!"

"Me?"

"Yes, you!" He pinched her on the nose. "You're quite a distraction, you know. Hurry! Let's get out of here."

She hurried into the skiff. Within minutes it seemed, the heavy cloud had blotted out the sun, darkening the day. Great shafts of lightning streaked through the sky, and thunder roared. The wind had risen, and great waves engulfed them as they made their way to the boat. Only a few minutes before she had been pleasantly warm. Now she was chilled to the bone. And scared.

That is, she would have been scared, if she hadn't seen Jake's strong fingers gripping the oars, winning the battle with the wind and waves. The same fingers that had pinched her nose, sending a thrill zinging through her.

"Hold this!" Jake's sharp voice broke into her thoughts and she grabbed the tie and held tight as he secured the skiff, then helped her climb aboard.

As she reached the deck, she realized she was being pounded by rain as well as seawater, and it was hard to keep her footing as the *Bluebird* was also being tossed by the high waves. Strong arms wound around her, as Jake, almost lifting her, led her down to her cabin.

"You're shivering. Take a hot shower," he said. "You'll find a robe somewhere. Anyway, the bed's the safest place to be in this."

"You...?" She hesitated, hating to see him go.

"Hot shower, too. But I'll come back and check on you. I think...I'll check the radio, but it's a pretty hefty storm. Go on now. Get in the shower."

She balanced herself in the little stall, feeling the

hot water pour through her hair and soak into her skin. Remembering...the feel of Jake's wet skin close to hers as he helped her across the deck, the touch of strong gentle fingers on her nose, the vibrations that had spun through her body.

She almost fell, putting on the terry-cloth robe she found, so she sat on the bed to towel her hair. She was curiously undisturbed by the violent rocking of the boat. Undisturbed by the jumble of sounds...the drumming of the rain, the wash of the waves against the boat, the ominous rumble of thunder. Every sound was drowned out by the memory of his words... "You are quite a distraction."

A distraction. That meant something, didn't it? Maybe not fascinating or beautiful or anything like that. But that did mean he did think about her, didn't it?

A rap on the door made her heart leap. "Are you decent?" Jake called.

"Yes. Come in."

He came in, managing to stay upright with the rolling gait of a born sailor. "Are you all right?" He had showered, too, and hadn't quite dried his hair. It was a little slick and a lock was falling forward. He brushed it back with the sleeve of his pullover. He was really a beautiful man.

"Hungry?" he asked.

"Not really." She hadn't thought about food, only about him. She stood up to take the bag he held out.

"Well, you might be later."

"Later?"

"Looks like we might be here for the night," he said. "The storm's set in for a spell. I think it's better to stay put than to try to ride it out. Okay?"

"You're the captain, sir."

"Good girl. Here, take this. Just cheese, crackers, and a couple of cans of soda. Put it in that drawer," he directed. "Else it'll fall all over."

"You think of everything, don't you?" she said, as she did as instructed. "Always prepared?"

"Not quite. Can't fix anything hot cause everything's sliding all... Hey, steady there!" He caught her just in time to prevent her falling. Caught her and held on.

Or maybe it was she who held on. Mesmerized by a pair of deep sea blue eyes. She clung to him, trying to overcome the giddy light-headed feeling, the pounding in her ears.

"Hey, don't be scared," he said, pulling her closer. "That's just thunder."

Thunder? She thought it was the pounding of her heart.

"Scared?" he asked again, brushing back her hair and looking down at her.

"No," she said, inherently honest.

"You'll be all right?"

"No." Not if he left. "Please...don't go. Stay with me," she whispered.

He looked doubtful. "I don't think...that might not be such a good idea." But there was hunger in his eyes. Hunger and something else…something wonderful that pulled her like a magnet. She reached up to touch one finger to his lips.

He gasped. "Judy…what do you want?"

She didn't know what she wanted. She had never before in her life felt this way. Something opened within her, something that had to be shared…by this man. "I want you to kiss me," she said.

The kiss was so sweet, so tender, so overwhelmingly passionate that it reached her very soul…awakening, beckoning, confirming.

Yes, oh, yes! This is what I want, she thought, as he took her to bed. She heard the whistle of the wind, the rain, and thunder of the storm outside. It was nothing. Only a vague overture to the storm of erotic yearning that engulfed her. A passionate hunger to be shared, enjoyed, assuaged with this man in the magic spell of this moment.

CHAPTER FIVE

THE storm was over. The firmly anchored *Bluebird* floated aimlessly, lazily, only rocking slightly in the aftermath of gentle waves. Washed clean by the rain, the blue and white vessel sparkled in the sun of early dawn that broke through clear skies to lighten the horizon. It poured through a porthole to touch the face of the sleeping woman.

She opened her eyes to the shaft of sunlight on blue walls. Heavenly blue.

"I'm in heaven…I'm in heaven…" Now she knew what the song meant. She was in heaven and she didn't want to move. She was still cradled in his arms, still aglow with happiness. Still filled with the wonder of what she had shared with this man.

This man. She studied the face of the man sleeping beside her. The lift of his brows, as if always raised in question. The curve of his full lips, always on the verge of a welcoming smile. The way he made you feel.

Comfortable. That was how she had felt from the moment she met him.

But… Comfortable? No. Nothing to do with how she had felt last night…the rush of passion that had shaken her to the roots. The torrent of sensations pulsing through her that turned her wild, eager, begging...pleading for she knew not what. The ecstasy was uncontrollable, but as natural as breathing. He had guided her to a peak of erotic pleasure she had never before experienced. In the throes of fulfillment, she had cried out, calling his name over and over again.

No, not comfortable. But natural. She snuggled closer, loving the feel of his body against hers. So right. Because...she loved him? Was that what made it right? The fondling, coupling, touching.

Touching. Ben. For the first time she understood. That was why he had absconded. He had known what she did not know. She didn't love him. I'm sorry, she thought, inwardly apologizing to the absent man. Poor Ben. But...thank you! I'm so glad you realized, and acted. She hoped he would find the right somebody.

As she had.

"Good morning."

"Good morning, yourself," she said, loving the way his eyes looked when he first opened them. Sleepy and dazed, as if not quite sure where he was or how he got there.

"Are...are you all right?" he asked, and now there was a flash of alarm in his eyes.

"Wonderful." Of course she was all right. Last night. And now...lying close to him, their bare skins touching.

"Are you sure?" She heard genuine concern in his voice. For her. How sweet. "You were..." He paused, as if reconsidering what he had started to say. "That was quite a storm, wasn't it?"

She nodded, smiling. It was nothing, compared to the tumult that had raged inside her.

He lifted a mop of her thick silky hair and seemed to study it. "You have lovely hair, Judy. In fact you are a beautiful desirable woman. Did I tell you that?"

"No." She shook her head, grinning. "All you said was that I was a distraction."

"Yes. A very tempting one." He was intent upon her hair, running his fingers through it, wrapping it around his hand. He did not take his eyes from it. "I know what you are going through. This has been a very difficult week for you. I didn't mean to take...to rush you. Things got a little hectic last night, and... Oh, hell, I lost my head!"

He was apologizing. For last night. For the most wonderful thing that had ever happened...

To her.

Not to him.

She had been thinking of forever, while he...

How stupid could she get! The way this man lived. This boat... Very convenient. For what probably happened most any night. Or several nights...with any woman.

A cold chill ran down her spine. For all she knew, he could be married. Or something. Mel. Whoever or whatever, indications were that she was a permanent fixture.

And you, Judy Taylor, are a one-night stand.

"Judy, I want you to know that—"

"Hush." She put a hand over his mouth. "Things can get spoiled by talk." She mustn't blame him. He had not come on to her. Not once. He had just been nice, rescuing her at the church, letting her stay here. It wasn't his fault that she had gone crazy last night. She had clung to him, begging, and…what happened. "You have been so kind. This week…the boat and everything, has meant so much to me. Did I ever say thank you?"

"About a dozen times."

"Well, I'm saying it again." She rolled away from him, out of bed. Picked up the robe from the floor and quickly wrapped it about herself. "But I did tell my mother I'd be home today. Hadn't we better get going?"

He sat up. "Judy, we need to talk."

"No. What I need is a good cup of coffee. And, hey, I do make a mean omelet. Want to try it?"

He nodded, but looked, as he often did, like he was trying to figure her out.

"Coming up, just as soon as I get dressed. Coffee first, though. That's your job." She winked at him and escaped into the bathroom.

Her heart felt like lead, but she had to play it light. She didn't want him to feel guilty.

In the galley, Jake scooped coffee grounds into the pot, feeling guilty as hell. He had taken advantage of her.

From the very first, he had known the state she was in. He had seen the pills. And hadn't he watched her up and down moods all this week? Mostly up, he had to admit. One of the things he had liked about her. Plucky kid, determined not to let this terrible thing that had happened get the best of her. He liked that.

As a matter of fact, he liked everything about her. That cute perfectly rounded little figure. That beautiful mane of honey blond hair that had covered his chest this morning. The blue eyes. Not the most beautiful woman he had known, but Judy Taylor had more than beauty.

Not only pluck. A vitality and wholehearted enthusiasm that made her a fabulous partner in any activity. A certain innocence.

Innocence. Last night had been a first for her. He knew that. But that kiss. And she had come so willingly, almost begging him to take her.

He was struck by a thought. She hadn't slept with Ben. Saving it for the wedding night? Jesus, what the man must have gone through.

But last night... Had she turned to him on the rebound? Hurting from rejection? Trying to prove to herself that she was desirable?

He had taken advantage of her pain.

She had trusted him. Those wide blue eyes viewed everyone with such trust...everyone, even a con like Ben Cruz.

Jake sighed. He hadn't meant to rush her into anything she wasn't ready for. Oh, yes, he had been at-

tracted to her from the first. But he knew she was
vulnerable, and had deliberately kept his distance, no
matter how his arms had itched to hold her.

Then last night...

Even now he was not quite sure how it happened.

The kiss. A mistake. A torch to a fire that was being
stoked all week. No way could he let her go after that
kiss.

She had clung to him, so eager, and willing.

He was accustomed to women who went willingly
to his bed.

But last night was different. Real. A first for him,
too. As if he were as innocent and trusting as she.
More than sex. Much more. A true union of heart and
soul.

Oh, yeah? Today, one short week ago, her heart
and soul were pledged to another man. A woman like
Judy doesn't pledge lightly.

Jilted... Vulnerable...

He had thought last night as remarkable for her as
for him. But he had seen the pain in her eyes when
she turned from him this morning. Then she had become so...so deliberately casual.

Regretting? Remembering Ben?

Hell, he ought to tell her what a bastard Ben is.

But how to bring it up? The pleasure of the night
was the proper topic for the morning after. Certainly
not a past and lost love.

And why was he feeling so damn awkward! Next
mornings were never awkward for him. Why this one?

Why was he feeling like a schoolboy after his first experience?

And why was Miss Innocent prancing around like such experiences were routine for her? One thing on her mind...the ingredients for her damned omelet.

"I thought so," she said now as she peered into the fridge. "One pimento left. Just the touch we need." She went on talking as she chopped the pimento, onion, and bell pepper. She covered every frivolous inconsequential topic she could think of. If she stopped talking, she would cry. That she would not do. Last night had been the most wonderful thing that had happened to her. She wouldn't spoil it by making a fool of herself. "Here you are, sir, as promised," she said, sliding the omelet onto two plates. "Tell me. Isn't this positively the best omelet you ever tasted?"

He closed his eyes, sampling. "Hmm! Right. Maybe you can get on as breakfast chef at The Fisherman."

"I already have a job, thank you very much. First thing Monday. I'll have to work hard this weekend to be ready. So eat up and let's ship out, captain!"

"Right. Only..." he hesitated. "There is something we need to talk about, Judy. Something I think you should understand."

She stiffened. He was going to apologize. She couldn't stand that.

"Did you love Ben Cruz very much?" he asked.

The relief was so great she almost laughed. "No. No indeed. And after..." She stopped. Last night had shown her what love could be like. But she couldn't say that. "I realize now that I never loved him."

"But…" He had that trying-to-figure-her-out look again. "You were going to kill yourself. Those pills…"

Now she did laugh. "Is that what you thought? Is that why you knocked them out of my hand?" She shook her head. "Aspirin. My head was pounding like crazy, and I thought—"

"But if you didn't love him…" The blue eyes were boring into hers now, searching, intense. "Why were you going to marry him?"

"Money!" She spit the word out like a bitter seed.

"Oh." It hit him hard.

"He was looking into the construction business and my stepfather asked me to be nice to him."

"*Be nice to him*." "Marry *him*."

For a measly two hundred and fifty thousand of *my* money? Jesus!

"Ben is very rich, you know."

"Oh?"

She nodded. "My mother kept saying how lucky I was, that it was such a good match. And—" she stopped. No use blaming it on her parents. She had been impressed, hadn't she? "Of course I knew it was, and… Oh, please, could we just not talk about it?"

He didn't want to talk about it. He knew about money. And what people would do for it.

CHAPTER SIX

FACING her mother was hard.

Alicia stood before her, the thin lips tight. "How could you? How could you?"

Not sure of what she was being accused, Judy faltered, "I only—"

"Stopped the marriage...right there at the church in front of everybody."

"*I* stopped it?"

"Everything so beautifully arranged." Alicia's voice broke. "Oh, how could you?"

"Mother, I did not stop the wedding. It was Ben. He didn't show. Remember?"

"You sent him away."

"No!"

"Yes! I thought so at first. I knew it when you ran away. Leaving us to face the music!"

"I'm sorry. I just needed to...to get away." Yes, she had run.

"Oh, it was horrible," Alicia wailed. "People sympathizing to your face, and grinning behind your back."

"Mother, nobody... People aren't like that."

"You don't know! You weren't there. You didn't see the smirk on Leanda Saunders's face! I have never been so humiliated in my life!'' Alicia sank onto the sofa, covering her face.

"I'm sorry.'' Judy bit her lip. She had been selfish, thinking only of herself, her relief. Actually enjoying herself! Never once thinking of what her mother was going through. "But…I never said one word to Ben. I had no idea he was going to…was not going to be there.'' She moved to put an arm around Alicia. "Mother, you must believe—''

Alicia stood up, knocking her arm away. "Didn't you try to get me to cancel the wedding just two days before?''

"Well, yes, I did, but—''

"You certainly did!'' Alicia stepped forward, glaring at her. "Coming on with all that foolishness…he wasn't the right man for you. You didn't love him!''

"All right! All right!'' Judy was suddenly angry. "I didn't love him. I don't. And I'm glad he didn't show. That we didn't get married. There! Are you satisfied?''

"Quite!'' Alicia gave her a nasty look. "Confession is good for the soul isn't it?''

"Look, I told you I didn't want to marry him. But I never said it to him. I never even hinted that—''

"Clever girl. But you still managed to get your feelings across, didn't you?''

That cut deep. She may be right, Judy thought. Maybe my actions spoke louder than words.

Her silence seemed to increase Alicia's wrath. "Oh, he got your signals all right. Ben Cruz is no fool," she said. "In fact, he's about the smartest richest man that'll ever come your way. You're the loser."

"Oh, Mother, I—"

"Don't 'oh, Mother' me! You're not the only loser. When Ben canceled the wedding, he canceled out on us, too. We're ruined!"

"Ruined? What do you mean?"

"I mean that Jim was counting on the money your intended was going to put into the business."

"Yes. I knew that."

"Did you know that since you didn't marry him, Ben did not invest? Jim has been forced into bankruptcy?"

"I didn't know things were that bad."

"Did you know that his creditors are crawling all over us? The IRS has taken over all his holdings, and he's going crazy trying to figure how we can come out of this. How we can survive? We've got nothing, Judy! Nothing! Jim's putting the house up for sale."

"Oh, I'm so sorry."

"Sorry, huh? So sorry you ran off to have yourself a nice vacation, huh?"

"No. I didn't. I..." She stopped. Wasn't that exactly what she had done?

"Left us to pick up the pieces, didn't you? Well, there are no pieces to pick up, young lady! Nothing! How do you like that?" Alicia burst into tears, ran to her own bedroom, and slammed the door.

Judy stood quite still, feeling chastened. Guilty.

Had she done this to them? What her mother said was at least partially true. If Ben had sensed how she felt…

She took a deep breath, lifted her shoulders. No use crying over spilt milk, even if she had knocked it over. What could she do now? Her mother always made things sound worse than they were. She would talk to Jim. She had reached home in the late afternoon and he hadn't yet come home. Where was he? And what was he doing if there were no pieces to pick up?

When she heard his pickup truck come around the house, she ran out the back door to greet him. He jumped down from the truck and held out his arms. "You're back! Boy, am I glad to see you. Are you all right?" he asked, his eyes full of concern.

"Oh, Jim." She flung herself into his protective arms. Not once had her mother asked about her. "I'm fine, Jim. Just fine," she said to reassure him. Then, inherently honest, "You know I didn't want to marry him, anyway."

"Yeah, we kinda pushed you into that one, didn't we?" he said, as they both settled onto the bench that surrounded the oak tree, their favorite conversation spot.

"Not really. I—"

"Yes, we did. My fault, Judy. I was so damned scared." He pulled a pack from his shirt pocket to select a cigarette.

"You shouldn't smoke, Jim."

"I don't. Just when I'm under a little stress."

"Like you are now. It's all my fault. Mother says—"

"Don't you believe it! This was coming on even before I ran into Ben. He was going to get more out of it than he was putting in, which was only a stop-gap anyway. I'd been extending myself far too much." Alicia, Judy thought. She always seemed to want far more than he could provide. "Business," he said, as if reading her thoughts. "Guess I got too big for my britches. Bought several properties in Richmond's East End."

"But...isn't that a slum area?"

"Worst ever. Thing is, I had a scoop. Thought I did anyway. Somebody put a bug in my ear that the powers that be were planning to dump a pile to upgrade that section."

"And?"

"Still just a rumor. And I've paid for a pile of rundown shacks."

"Oh, Jim."

"Oh, I still have hope. Upgraded, that section would become prime property, and somebody in city hall is bound to see that."

That was Jim. Always the optimist. "I hope...*think* you're right," she said, crossing her fingers.

"And when they do, you'll be sitting pretty, Judy."

"Me?"

"It's all yours, squirt. Even before Cruz turned up, I could see the break coming. So I transferred all the

East End properties to you, in your real name, Judy Crenshaw. Yours. Not mine, or your mother's in any sense whatever. You see?''

''No, I don't. Why would you transfer property to me?''

''Because you don't owe anybody anything. I even paid cash for your Volkswagen. Nobody can take anything away from you.''

''I still don't see—''

''How would you like to start your own construction company?''

Her eyes opened wide, and he grinned at her. ''Crenshaw Construction.''

''But I couldn't. I mean…I'd have to have a contractor's license.''

''Piece of cake. Like it was planned when you decided to study architecture. Didn't you tell me your first courses had mostly to do with construction…structure and materials?''

She nodded.

''So you have the basics. And you must have picked up on something those summers you worked with me.''

Again she nodded.

''We'll study a bit, but I'm sure you can pass the test.'' He talked on, while Judy, in a bit of a daze, listened.

''Think of it, squirt. Your own. Crenshaw Construction. Nothing to do with Taylor Construction. I'll be your employee. And nothing illegal about it. As a matter of fact, I intend to pay my creditors and square things with the IRS as soon as I get back on my feet. But I have to have something to work with to do it. Understand?''

"You are cold-blooded, Judy," Celia Myers declared three weeks later, as she secured the addressed envelope to the top of the sealed package. "It's killing me to see you send back all of these beautiful gifts."

"Poor, poor baby." Judy chuckled. "So sweet of you to help me while you suffer."

"Well, you're sure not suffering. Honestly, Judy, I would die of mortification if I were left at the altar by a beautiful hunk like Ben Cruz!"

"You don't have to remind me. Mother does that every day. Believe me, I am suffering," Judy said, as she placed another package on the floor to be delivered to UPS.

"Nonsense. It's like you never even heard of Ben Cruz."

"I told you. Ben and I were a mistake. I'm just lucky he realized it."

Celia ran a hand through her short curly hair and regarded her friend. "Guess so. You sure don't look heartbroken."

Little you know, Judy thought. This heavy feeling, like a stone in her chest, could be heartbreak, couldn't it? It got heavier by the day as hope faded, a little each day. Hope for just one little phone call.

Jake Mason did not call.

Her instincts had been right. As far as he was concerned, she was a one-night stand.

It hurt. The fabulous week...the night she would never forget. It had meant so much to her.

So little to him.

Why couldn't she get him out of her mind! How could she miss him so much? She hardly knew him.

Wrong. Her cheeks flushed hot. She knew him better than she had ever known any man. She wasn't sorry. She wasn't! It had been...a beautiful, wonderful, exhilarating—

"Hey!" Celia snapped her fingers under her nose. "Where are you?"

"Trying to think what to say," she lied, as she hurriedly scribbled a note. "You don't want to say the same thing to everybody, even though you are just returning a gift."

"Guess so," Celia said. "So you're not taking your old job back?"

"No. I'm working with Dad. And studying. Which is why I'm just now getting the last of these gifts off. But I passed!"

"Passed what?"

"The contractor's test. You are now looking at a genuine licensed building contractor!"

"What! You're a contractor? A pint-sized gal like you? What can you do?"

"Lots. You forget. I used to work for Dad in the summer. I already know how to paint and hang wallpaper. And fetch, carry, and hold," she said, laughing. "If things don't get too heavy."

Celia gave her a dubious look. "Building a house is a heck of a lot different than designing one, you know."

"More alike than different. I'd never have passed my contractor's test if I hadn't studied architecture."

And what she had learned was proving to be very handy right now, she thought, as she donned jeans and boots the next morning, and headed for work. During the summers she had worked for him, she had simply followed instructions. Now, with two years of architecture behind her, she could understand why his business was in a slump. He wasn't keeping up.

Taylor Construction had always been a relatively small company. Jim had maintained a small staff, and, in the earlier years, building only single houses or small apartment complexes. Lately, the major portion, almost all, of his business was repairs, mostly on houses he had built. This time, in the few days she had worked with him, they had replaced the tile in one house, refinished the kitchen cabinets in another. In both houses, Judy's trained eye had noted places where modern innovations would greatly improve the appearance and up the market value. She was waiting for a good opportunity to voice some of her ideas to Jim.

Perhaps, she thought, when they talked about what to do with the houses he had transferred to her.

Bought cheap, he explained. "They're falling apart and in such a bad location."

She gave him a dubious look. "They don't sound, and I quote, like 'the houses that will rebuild your fortune.'"

"Trust me, kid." He winked. "I told you about that rumor."

"Which," she couldn't help reminding him, "is still a rumor." But Jim would not be daunted, and she found herself catching his enthusiasm. She hadn't yet seen the houses, but she knew they were a slightly earlier version of the ones they were currently repairing. Couldn't be much different, she decided, and spent each night thumbing through her architect books and current pamphlets on "blending the best of the old with the best of the new." She was bursting with ideas, and used every opportunity to try them out.

"You're a marvel, Judy," Jim told her. "Sanson just wanted a new tub, and you've got us redoing his whole bathroom! If you keep this up, we'll have to hire another worker."

"Not 'till when *and if* Richmond comes through! We're not out of the woods yet."

"You're tough, Ms. Crenshaw." Jim sat back on the roof and made an exaggerated gesture of wiping sweat from his brow. "I'm plumb tuckered."

"No complaints! We're working, aren't we?" Judy grinned at him. She was glad they were working hard. Glad she fell asleep over her books. Glad she was too exhausted to think.

He hadn't even acknowledged her note.

Did he get it?

Anyway, she was glad that he didn't call.

Glad that even if he did call, she wouldn't see him. Too busy during the day, and too tired at night.

All right...*truth*! *She had lost her heart, and his had not been touched. Best for them both if she never saw him again.*

Jake Mason stood in the master bedroom of his more than adequate home, and read the note again.

"Dear Jake, I'm saying it again. Thank you. And thanks to your lovely *Bluebird* who gave me the inspiration and confidence I sorely needed. I may not fly, but now I can at least sail on my own. My gratitude and all good wishes to you both. Judy."

The note had arrived two days after she left it in care of Sims, who had forwarded it to his home. No reference to the enclosed check, but he knew it was payment for the money he had given her. His first impulse had been to tear it to shreds. But then...it was in her handwriting, tiny and precise letters, as perfectly shaped as she. Imprinted was her address and phone number. He would know where to get in touch.

If he wanted to get in touch.

He put the note in his desk drawer. Out of sight. Out of mind.

Her words haunted him. "I never loved Ben. It was the money."

I've got a hell of a lot more money than Ben Cruz. So? She's proposing?

Women don't propose. They have a hundred different ways of getting what they want.

And you know them all, huh?

Let's just say I recognize a come-on. She had whispered, "Please don't leave me." She had wrapped her arms around him, pressed her lips to his, practically begging him to take her.

Not like a Little Miss Innocent, huh?

But a come-on just the same. And I thought... I didn't think. I lost my head.

Did you lose your heart?

The thought frightened him. He couldn't forget her words... "It was the money." He had the money that Ben Cruz never had or would ever get.

She had been so loving, so yielding. Women who pretended love for him when it was really for his money made him feel cheap.

He had lost his heart only once. To Lisa, who was now married to Scot, his best friend... Lisa said he never loved her, and maybe she was right. He had never felt as close, as kin to her, as, in just one week, he had felt toward Judy. Not just the sex thing, either. It was... Well, he didn't want to think about that.

"You thought you loved me," Lisa said, "because I was the only woman who admitted to wanting to marry you on account of your money."

True. He had liked her blatant honesty.

"I never loved Ben. It was the money."

That was honest, wasn't it?

True.

Try a little honesty yourself, chum. You couldn't get enough of her, could you? That last night was inevitable. If she hadn't opened her arms, you would have opened yours.

He took out the check, found the phone number. Dialed.

The phone rang and rang. No answer.

In a couple of hours he would be on his way to Bolivia. It was to be a two-week rafting trip traversing the water channels of the wild unexplored areas of the Bolivian Andes. Exciting. Dangerous. He was looking forward to it.

He would call her when he returned.

Maybe.

CHAPTER SEVEN

JUDY did not go with Jim to the Richmond City Council meeting the night they were to vote on the East End project. She tried to wait up for him, but, as usual, fell asleep over her books. At breakfast next morning, he waved the newspaper at her.

"It's fact now, Judy. The rumor is fact!"

"That's wonderful! You were right, Jim."

"Ye'. Listen to this." He read the detailed account of the council's unanimous vote guaranteeing home improvement loans on any East End property to any qualified owner.

"What does that mean?" Alicia asked.

"It means we're in the money, honey. We own four houses down there, which, when upgraded, will bring in a tidy sum."

"And we'll probably get contracts for upgrading others," Judy said. "It looks promising."

"Damn right, it's promising. We're in the right spot, at the right time, squirt."

She was excited, already toying with ideas. The district could become, well, not as plush as Georgetown, but certainly upper class enough for the middle bracket of government and commercial employees. *Very promising.*

The houses were an hour's drive from Elmwood, and it was several days before she saw them. They were busy trying to finish up on their other commitments.

The day came that Thursday. It was raining cats and dogs, and they had to stop work on a new roof they were replacing. "A good day," Jim said. "To take a look at your houses."

"Mine!" she echoed. "You know they're yours, Jim."

"Yours, Ms. Crenshaw Construction, and don't you forget it!" He grinned. "You want to qualify for that hunk of upgrading money, don't you?"

Maybe this is a good day to look over the district, she thought, as Jim maneuvered his truck through gutted and sometimes flooded streets. No gangs or loafers hanging out in this pouring rain. Maybe hiding out in some of these boarded-up houses, she thought with some alarm. And was somewhat relieved to see a lone woman in a hooded raincoat hurry into what looked like a grocery store, while two leather-jacketed youngsters disappeared into a pool hall.

As they traversed the area, she could see the potential. It was rundown of course, small deteriorating houses, with junk or old cars piled in the yards. But reminiscent of old grandeur with large trees and pretty good-sized lawns. It could be fantastic!

Jim stopped in front of one of the boarded-up houses, reached into a locked container and took out a heavy bunch of keys. "Okay, squirt, let's go."

Not bothering with an umbrella, they rushed down a broken walk and up some rickety steps to stand on a sheltered porch. Not very sheltered, however. As Jim fumbled with the padlock, rain poured through in several spots.

But Judy saw more than a leaking roof. A real honest-to-goodness old-fashioned front porch. She pictured a quiet little township from a bygone era with front porches and large front lawns. Quaint. Different.

Jim finally opened the door, and they stepped in. The first thing Judy felt was an unexpected warmth after the outside chill. Musty, but warm and welcoming until—

"All right, mother! Get the hell out of here. This is my space!" He stood before them, tall, big and menacing. Wielding a heavy two-by-four.

Judy stepped back, a paralyzing wave of fear flooded through her, turning her knees to jelly.

Jim stood his ground. "What do you mean...*your* space. You're trespassing, buddy."

"Jim..." Judy pulled on his sleeve, her eyes on the big man, the club in his hand, the closed door behind him. There could be others. "Please. We'd better go, Jim."

"Oh, no! He's the one to go. And now! He's a squatter. He has no right to be here. And I'm calling the cops." Jim grabbed Judy by the hand to leave.

"Nah you ain't!" The man leaped in front of them, and slammed the wood butt on the floor with such force that the whole house shook, and the startled cries of a baby came from the direction of the closed door. The squatter brandished the club, striking the floor again, and blocking their way.

"No, Charlie! Don't!" The anguished voice was heard behind the closed door. The door opened and a young woman came out, carrying the crying baby in her arms. "Don't fight, Charlie. Let's just go."

"Go where, baby?" the man choked with anger and despair. He raised the club in disgusted resignation.

Jim saw it as an attack. He raised his arms in defense, but was suddenly stricken with a seizure. He fell to the floor, gasping for air.

Judy dropped to her knees beside him, and screamed, "Oh, God! You killed him."

"Get out of the way, lady." Charlie pushed her aside. "He's having a heart attack." He immediately commenced the rhythmic pumps used in the heart resuscitation maneuver. Pumping. Counting. Opening his mouth and blowing air into Jim's lungs, mouth to mouth. "Twelve...thirteen...fourteen...fifteen," he breathed, pausing only once to shout, "Call an ambulance, lady!"

Judy ran to the truck, and called. When she returned, she saw with relief that Jim's eyes were open and he was breathing on his own.

It seemed ages, but it must have been within minutes that the medical team arrived and took over. They watched as the paramedics placed Jim on a stretcher. "I hope he's going to be all right." The man named Charlie looked apologetic, and scared. He turned to Judy. "I'm sorry. I know this is my fault."

Judy touched his hand. "Your fault that he's alive. Thank you."

"But if I hadn't...I didn't mean to set him off. Look, I'm sorry," he said again. "We'll get out right away."

"No. You and your family stay put...please," she added. "I want to talk to you later," she said, as she got into the truck and followed the ambulance.

One week after the massive heart attack, Jim was holding his own.

But just barely. "We can't do a bypass until we get his blood pressure down," the doctor had said.

That could take forever, Judy thought, if something wasn't done to calm his state of mind.

She pulled her chair closer to his hospital bed and took his hand. "Everything is going just fine, Jim," she said.

He shook his head. "You two would be better off, if I had kicked the bucket."

"Oh, will you shut up with that kind of talk!"

"Well, at least you'd have my insurance money."

"And why would we need that? With all that home improvement money just waiting. Remember?"

"Not with me laying up here on my back, honey. You can't take on all that by yourself."

"Ha! A lot of faith you have in Crenshaw Construction."

Jim tried to smile. "I don't want to put you down, squirt. You're the greatest. But by yourself... It's too much." He sighed. "We didn't even finish Donaldson's roof. Poor Alicia. She must be worried sick."

"Alicia's just fine. She'll be in later." Her mother had been banned from Jim's room because her tears upset him. She had been asked to remain in the waiting room. "And we have finished the roof! Would you like to see the check?" She grinned, seeing his eyes widen as she held the check before him.

"But how did you? Did you call Todd?" he asked, mentioning one of his old employees.

"Not Todd. Charlie."

"Charlie?"

"Remember the squatter?"

"Oh, that big son of a—"

"Calm down, Jim." She pushed him back upon his pillows. "He saved your life. He was the one who recognized you were having a heart attack, and he immediately went into action. He gave you first aid, and made me call an ambulance. And wait!" She held up a hand. "He's a gold mine. A real find. I went back the next day to talk with him. He wasn't there, but his wife was, and she told me about their streak of bad luck. He lost his job when that canning plant closed down about a year ago. He'd been doing a few odd jobs, but they had used up all their savings and were evicted from their apartment two months ago, and...well, you know."

"Yeah. Squatting on my property!"

"Wait!" Again she held up a hand. "You wouldn't believe the repairs he has made to your property! His wife showed me."

He stared in amazement as she detailed the improvements. "All that?" he asked.

"All that. He's a real handyman, can do almost anything. He's working with me now for the minimum wage and free lodging...that is, if you don't mind, Jim?"

"You're asking me? It's your house. And your company, Ms. Crenshaw." He squeezed her hand. "Looks like you know what you're doing, squirt."

"Jim is looking much better," Judy told her mother a few minutes later. "He'll probably be up to the surgery soon."

This was not much comfort to Alicia. "Oh, God, the surgery!" she said, putting away her book of meditations. "I couldn't stand it if anything went wrong. If anything happens to Jim."

"Nothing's going to happen to him, except what will make him stronger." Judy put an arm around her mother. She was beginning to understand that Alicia couldn't help the way she was. She was too tense, too worried about everything, and needed reassurance just as Jim did. "Why don't we stop for a bite to eat before I take you home? That way, you won't have to bother with cooking."

The days flew by as if on wings. She was so busy. Between the hospital, her mother, and work.

Work. Plenty of it. The Donaldsons had been pleased with the new roof, and when Judy mentioned dormer windows....

"Yes!" Mrs. Donaldson had been delighted. She had been wondering how to get in more light.

Judy was delighted, too. Better lighting was one of the most needed innovations in those old houses, and it could be easily accomplished with larger windows, skylights, and the new electrically controlled indirect lighting.

It seemed one job followed another. The Jacksons, next door to the Donaldsons, had turned over their house to the son's family, and he wanted to turn the attic into another bedroom and a playroom for the children. Of course, Judy said, wondering how she could fit the job in.

Then Todd, Jim's regular electrician, hit a dull streak, and was glad to hook up with Judy. "You're getting to be as good a businessman as your old man," he told Judy.

"Businesswoman," she corrected.

"That's what I said," Todd grunted. "Want me to contact Leo? He did all Jim's plumbing, and the Days across the street, are thinking of adding a Jacuzzi."

"Yes, contact him," she said. She needed to build up a crew. She had enough jobs to do so now, and she had already filed an application for a home improvement loan on Charlie's house, which she intended to use as a model to attract other contracting jobs. Funny how she thought of it as "Charlie's

house.'' Maybe he could afford to buy it, if she took
a second for the down. She liked Charlie, and he was
proving to be invaluable. He always seemed to know
what needed to be done, and often how to do it. Once
she asked him how he knew so much about the building trade and he said, ''Three years in Uncle Sam's
Engineering Corps. We built everything from barracks
to bridges.''

Thank you, Uncle Sam, she thought. She needed a
right-hand man, and he was it, overseeing works in
progress while she was in and out, between visits to
the hospital. Jim's surgery, a three-way bypass was
successful, thank God, and he was slowly recuperat-
ing in the hospital. More at ease, however. He was so
proud and so relieved that things were going well. She
felt that at last she was repaying him in some measure
for all his years of support.

Her mother also leaned heavily upon her. It was as
if she had been affected by her husband's illness, be-
coming frail and helpless. Because she had always
been so dependent upon him, Judy realized, and was
glad now to lend her own support. She couldn't re-
press a little surge of guilt.

If she had married Ben, none of this would have
happened. His money might have saved the business,
prevented Jim's heart attack, her mother's lapse.

If…? Oh, for goodness' sake, it was Ben who absconded!

But did she cause it? Give out the wrong signal?

Oh, for goodness' sake, that was over. She was

making up for it, wasn't she? She was building up the business, which was making Jim better, which was making her mother better. And she was having fun doing it!

Days spent on a little cruiser called the *Bluebird* seemed long ago and far away the afternoon that she left the hospital and headed for the Jacksons', where Charlie was finishing the wainscotting on the attic room.

"That looks great," she said, admiring his neat work. "I think that map-of-the-world wallpaper will fit nicely. Better check the measurements again." She took out her measuring tape, jumped on a stepladder, reached up.

It hit her all at once, the wave of sickness, the dizziness. If Charlie hadn't caught her, she would have fallen to the floor.

When she opened her eyes, he was mopping her face with a paper towel he had dipped in cold water.

She sat up. "I'm all right." Still a little queasy, but all right. Charlie looked so scared, she grinned at him. "We Taylors must be allergic to you, Charlie. We always fall out when you're around."

"And scare the hell out of me. Look, hadn't you better see a doctor?"

"I'm fine. I had lunch with Mother at the hospital. I think that chicken sandwich didn't agree with me."

"But you got sick at lunch yesterday, remember? You could be coming down with something, like that stomach flu that's going 'round."

"I can't come down with anything," she cried in alarm. "This is absolutely the worst time for me to be sick. We've got too many things going right now, and Jim's still in the hospital."

"I know." The tall man she had come to depend upon looked concerned. "Maybe you'd better go home and get some rest. I'll finish up here."

"I couldn't rest. I'd be too busy thinking."

"Well, maybe you could get something to settle your stomach. May's stomach was always upset when she was pregnant with Chuckie, and the doctor gave her something that checked it right away."

She stared at him. She'd better see a doctor.

It couldn't be true. It couldn't! This was the worst possible time.

She looked at Dr....Allen? No...Alden. She hadn't gone to her regular doctor for fear it might be true.

It was true.

What was she to do?

NO RISK, NO OBLIGATION TO BUY...NOW OR EVER!

GUARANTEED

PLAY "ROLL A DOUBLE" AND YOU GET FREE GIFTS! HERE'S HOW TO PLAY:

1. Peel off label from front cover. Place it in space provided at right. With a coin, carefully scratch off the silver dice. Then check the claim chart to see what we have for you – FOUR FREE BOOKS and a mystery gift – ALL YOURS! ALL FREE!

2. Send back this card and you'll receive brand-new Harlequin Romance® novels. These books have a cover price of $3.25 each, but they are yours to keep absolutely free.

3. There's no catch. You're under no obligation to buy anything. We charge nothing – ZERO – for your first shipment. And you don't have to make any minimum number of purchases – not even one!

4. The fact is, thousands of readers enjoy receiving books by mail from the Harlequin Reader Service®. They like the convenience of home delivery...they like getting the best new novels BEFORE they're available in stores...and they love our discount prices!

5. We hope that after receiving your free books you'll want to remain a subscriber. But the choice is yours – to continue or cancel any time at all! So why not take us up on our invitation, with no risk of any kind You'll be glad you did!

The Harlequin Reader Service® — Here's how it works

Accepting free books places you under no obligation to buy anything. You may keep the books and gift and return the shipping statement marked "cancel." If you do not cancel, about a month later we'll will send you 6 additional novels, and bill you just $2.67 each plus 25¢ delivery per book and applicable sales tax, if any. That's the complete price – and compared to cover prices of $3.25 each – quite a bargain! You may cancel at any time, but if you choose to continue, every month we'll send you 6 more books, which you may either purchase at the discount price...or return to us and cancel your subscription.
*Terms and prices subject to change without notice. Sales tax applicable in N.Y.

If offer card is missing write to: Harlequin Reader Service, 3010 Walden Ave., P.O. Box 1867, Buffalo, NY 14240-1867

BUSINESS REPLY MAIL
FIRST-CLASS MAIL   PERMIT NO. 717   BUFFALO, NY

POSTAGE WILL BE PAID BY ADDRESSEE

HARLEQUIN READER SERVICE
3010 WALDEN AVE
PO BOX 1867
BUFFALO NY 14240-9952

NO POSTAGE
NECESSARY
IF MAILED
IN THE
UNITED STATES

CHAPTER EIGHT

HE SAT in the bar, the martini before him untouched, his eyes focused on the entry. He knew he was early. But he could hardly wait to see her.

Why?

Because he couldn't get her out of his mind. Even in that wild otherworld where he had been for the last few weeks, she was there. Her musical laughter echoed over the rush of tumbling waters as he'd whirled through the rapids of a narrow Bolivian gorge. The bright luster of a star, a reminder of clear blue eyes. Even the symphony of bird calls evoked a memory. "I feel like a bird. I could fly."

Strange how he remembered everything she'd said. A woman he had known for only one short week, and not all of that week. One night.

A woman he couldn't forget. He wanted to tell her, share with her, hear the laughter and see the wonder in her eyes. He'd meant to call her as soon as he got in.

He was pleased that she had called him. "A week ago," Sims said. "She asked that you get in touch with her as soon as you returned. Here's the phone number."

The same number that was on her check, he noted, surprised that he had memorized it.

"Jake! Oh, thank you for calling." She sounded relieved. Had she not expected him to return her call?

"Thank you," he said. "Sims said you called when I was in Bolivia."

"Yes. I need…that is, I would like to see you."

"Good. I would like very much to see you. When? And what, by the way, is your address? I could come—"

"No!" A sharp exclamation, a deep breath, and then, determinedly calm. "I have to be in Wilmington tomorrow. On business," she added, almost as an afterthought. "Could we meet someplace? About one? Would that be convenient?"

"Fine," he said. They agreed to meet for lunch at Aldo's.

Ten after one. She was late. Business? What kind of business in Wilmington?

One-fifteen. His impatient glance surveyed the entry way again and again. One-thirty.

And…there she was! Shoulders erect, head lifted, that golden mass of hair swinging. Something about her stance. Determined, almost militant. The way she looked when she dumped that wedding finery in the bin.

He had been watching her so intently, he hadn't moved. But when he saw her approach the maître d', he rushed forward. "Hello, Judy. I was waiting in the bar."

"Oh. Hello." she smiled, but her lips trembled, and there was something apprehensive about the way she looked at him. "How...how are you? And how was your trip?"

"Fine. I reserved a table, but..." He gestured toward the bar. "Would you like a drink first?"

"Oh, yes, that would be..." She broke off, shaking her head. "No. Better not. I have to drive right back. I'm sorry that I'm late," she said as they were seated. "They're moving Jim to a convalescent home in the morning, and I had to make arrangements."

"Jim?"

"My stepfather. He had open heart surgery."

"Oh, I'm sorry." He wondered if she needed help, but was reluctant to ask.

"Oh, it went well. He's fine. Just needs a few weeks to convalesce. My mother doesn't cope very well."

"I see. Is there anything I can do. Do you need—"

"Nothing, thank you. Jim's not the best of patients, but we're managing. But...I...there's something else." She halfheartedly poked at her salad, picked up her wineglass, put it down. "I have a bit of a problem. I need your help," she said. And was silent.

Why was she so nervous? He watched the rapid blinking of her eyes, saw tiny white teeth bite into her lower lip. Those same teeth had bitten into his skin that night when she had clung to him, calling his name over and over again. His body quivered with the memory. That stormy tumultuous, glorious, wonderful night. Why was she hesitant? Didn't she know he would do anything for her? "Anything," he said. "Just ask."

"I want you to marry me."

Surely this was some kind of joke. "My dear, this is so sudden," he quipped, and started to laugh. Checked it. This was no joke. She was dead serious.

"I'm pregnant."

"Pregnant?" He didn't have to say it. She read it in his eyes. *On a one-night stand? I haven't seen you in two months. Anything could have happened...with anyone!*

She swallowed. Of course he would expect details...proof. "My business today is with Dr. Alden, an obstetrician in this city. This is my second visit. He confirmed it on my first. I am now two months pregnant."

Romantic visions faded in the wake of the nightmare. Trapped. A nightmare he had always been careful to avoid. But that night...the boat rocking wildly in a raging storm, and a woman in his arms, a passionate desirable woman who smelled of lavender soap and sea water. She had clung to him and begged... Who the hell would think of condoms, which, in any case, were stored in his own cabin?

"Damn!"

"My sentiments exactly." The bitter edge to her voice was so unlike her that it shocked him. She softened it immediately, pleading, "Look, it needn't be so bad. It wouldn't be a real marriage, and certainly not a lasting one. Just until the baby is born, or my pregnancy well on the way. We could find ourselves incompatible at any time...six months or whatever you say. Divorce is easy."

And costly, he thought, remembering. "I didn't love Ben. It was the money."

"So what's the point?" he asked. "I'll pay. How much? For the baby, or for...whatever you intend to do. That's easy, too, you know."

Her face went white. "I don't intend to *do* anything, except have this baby, which happens to be yours. All I'm asking is that you help me gain a little respectability for—"

"Respectability! Now that's an old-fashioned word."

"Not to my mother, it isn't. It's as much a part of her as angels, morality, and marriage. It would kill her if I became an unwed mother."

"Oh?"

"Yes. And she's already been through so much. She was so happy, planning my wedding...so crushed by what happened, which she says was all my fault. Maybe it was. And now Jim's surgery, which is not quite over yet." She was biting her lip again. "I can't do this to her. I can't."

He refused to be moved. Damn if he'd let her get to him. "So this proposed marriage is for your mother. In that case, we could just *pretend* to be—"

"No." She was chewing so hard on her lip, he

thought it might bleed. "I want respectability for my child, too. Or call it legitimacy."

"Aha! Truth time! Your love for your child. Your desire that he, or she, shall have legal claim to my name and, incidentally of course, to my fortune."

She caught her breath, shocked by his words, the contempt in his face. Did he think she was after his money? That she had actually planned this to...to trap him? A hot flush of anger gripped her. "How dare you think such a thing? Why, you egotistical son of..." She heard movements from another table and was aware that her voice had risen.

"I didn't say you planned it."

"Funny. That's what I heard. Loud and clear." Not what she had expected from the kind man who had rescued her from the church that day. Tears burned her eyes, and she felt sick. She wouldn't be sick. Not now. She met his look, her eyes flashing. "But, hear this! I am not a murderer. I will not kill this baby, for your convenience nor mine!"

"I am not asking you to get rid of it. I am only saying that marriage is not necessary."

"The marriage is for my convenience. Conventionality. Respectability. Believe me, I thought of everything before approaching you. Of other means, taking a job in California or somewhere, until I have the child. But I can't leave now with Jim...all the business dependent upon me. Anyway, I'd still have to explain a child, my responsibility for life."

"Look, I told you I will pay—"

"My responsibility. Financial and otherwise. Have your lawyers print up one of those prenuptial agreements."

"Not worth the paper it's printed on if there is a child."

"I'll sign anything you wish. I wouldn't touch a penny of your precious money. And I'm not asking you to change your life. All I'm asking is that you marry me for a few short months."

"And if I refuse?"

"Then there's nothing more to be said. Thank you for lunch." She stood up quickly, fighting the sickness.

He grabbed her hand. "Wait, Judy. Let's talk this out."

"No. Never mind. Just forget it." She tried to pull away, to get out of there before all that she had eaten came up.

"No. You can't face this alone. I—"

"Pardon me. Lady, are you being harassed?" The man from the next table spoke to Judy, but his threatening look was focused on Jake, who glared back at him.

"No, thank you. Not harassed," Judy cried, desperately controlling the heaving. "Just dismissed," she added as Jake's hand loosened and she broke away.

"Wait, Judy." Jake brushed the man aside, followed, and watched her disappear into the ladies' room. Damn. He hadn't meant to upset her. He just wanted to clear things up.

Without involving yourself, huh?

Damn!

Well, you can't get 'round it. You know damn well the child is yours.

These days no woman gets pregnant unless she wants to.

Innocent, untouched? Maybe she's as trapped as you.

Maybe. But she's different.

Different?

Not like she appeared those long-ago days on the *Bluebird*.

Oh?

Maybe not different. "I never loved Ben. It was the money."

His child.

He looked at the closed door of the ladies' room. Was she ever coming out?

She bent over the toilet, as the vomit erupted again and again, tearing at her insides and emptying her stomach. When it was over, she leaned against the wall, feeling weak. Trying not to be bitter. What did she expect?

That week on the *Bluebird*, he had seemed so understanding, so kind, and—

A lot of difference between a week's berth on his boat, and a wedding band on your finger, stupid!

Okay, so I'm the stuckee, she thought, as she

washed her face and rinsed her mouth. And what do I do now?

Hey, these are modern times. Unwed mothers are pretty common.

Alicia!

Well... Judy looked down at her flat stomach. She probably wouldn't be showing for another three months. By that time, the business would be secure, Jim well enough to take over. Maybe she could go away, or...and...

Well, she had three months to figure it out. She put on fresh lipstick, combed her hair and lifted her shoulders.

She opened the outer door and bumped into him.

"Come on, Judy. Let's go someplace where we can talk."

Three days later, they were married in Atlantic City, by a justice of the peace, before two witnesses they did not know. Who would know that the ceremony had not occurred two months earlier?

"If I am going to live a lie, it will be a big one," Judy had declared. "I met you...somewhere, and fell passionately in love. I confessed to Ben the night before, and he...well, he said I was going to be the one to look like a fool, not him. I ran from the church to you and...and we married. Okay?"

"You expect somebody to swallow that pail of hogwash?"

"Then you think up a better one!" she snapped.

She was tired. They had arrived back at the Richmond Airport where they had met that morning for the flight to Atlantic City. They planned to drive immediately to Elmwood, where he would be introduced to her folks. Right now she was so tired, she didn't care whether they swallowed her story or not.

A flabbergasted Alicia swallowed it immediately. Jake Mason of Mason Enterprises! "Oh, I do understand. True love conquers all," she cooed. "My darling girl, you should have told me. I could have arranged everything. Oh, my! We must have a reception…just as soon as Jim recovers."

Jim, at the convalescent home, might have been skeptical, but was too doped up to question. Judy was relieved. "We don't even have to live together," she told Jake as they walked back to the car. "You could say you have to be on some long business trip, or out of the country for some urgent reason. They'd never know. I could live at home while—"

"The hell with that," he said. "I've got friends and relations, too, you know."

"So?"

"I'm damned if I'm going to look trapped! Maybe I also fell passionately in love. Get it?"

She got it. She agreed to move into the bedroom adjoining his, at his home, wherever that was. It would be a long commute, but she had to make some compromises, didn't she? "We'll have to go back to the house to pack a few things," she said, wondering why they hadn't planned these things before. Details got lost at shotgun weddings, she thought, as she added, "And we'll have to go back to the airport to pick up my Volkswagen." How had she forgotten that? It had been sitting there all day. What would the parking fee be?

He paid the fee, but suggested they might dump the car.

"No. I'll need it," she said. At two in the morning, they arrived at the palatial Mason estate in Wilmington Heights, the Volks did seem out of place beside the silver Porsche in the six-car garage.

"Look," he said as he pulled her suitcase from the trunk. "You don't have to drive this. You could use the Porsche or that Cad over there. Or, I'll buy whatever you like."

"The Volkswagen is fine."

"Oh? It's lopsided, and this fender is bashed, and—"

"It's mine," she said, trying not to sound as awed as she felt. This was where he lived? They must have driven through two acres of lawn to reach that huge garage and this huge house. How many rooms? she wondered, as he switched on a light in what was a small breakfast room.

"Would you like something to eat or drink?" He was being very polite, and for some reason that irritated her.

She shook her head, wondering if she would ever want to swallow another bite. All she wanted was somewhere where she could be alone and lie down.

And think. But first… "You…this is where you live? All by yourself?" That is, when he wasn't on the *Bluebird* or flying off to Brazil or somewhere.

"It's home. I've lived here all my life. My mother remained after the divorce, but spends most of her time at the villa in Italy."

"Oh, I see. And your father?" She was suddenly curious about him.

"Dead."

"Oh. I'm sorry."

"Ten years ago, but he had moved out before then. Anyway, I am not exactly alone. The Hunts live here. You'll meet them tomorrow. Come, I'll show you to your room."

CHAPTER NINE

SHE was not so tired that she was unaware. She saw at once that her jeans and heavy boots were out of place in the long mirrored closet as her Volks was in the garage. As she was in this room, three times the size of her own, and that was not counting the separate powder room, the separate bath with its deep sunken tub, and the patio seen through the sliding-glass doors. A woman's room, soft and feminine with its cushions and downy comforter, plush carpet, and sheer curtains. Even the colors were soft and feminine...a pale almost white lavender subtly blended with touches of deep rose.

She might have been overwhelmed by the luxury had she not been fascinated by the sheer beauty, enticed by the comfort. The closet was empty, toiletries in the powder and bath, available and unused. Just waiting...welcoming. She pushed aside all thought, and allowed the room to embrace her. She soaked in a scented bubble bath in the big tub and fell asleep in the down cushions of the queen-sized bed, as if she had not a care.

At four-thirty the next morning, however, she took off the glass slippers and donned the boots. She saw no one as she made her way down to the garage, and got into her Volkswagen for the drive to Virginia. She couldn't afford to miss one day's work, and she wanted to get on the road before the heavy traffic.

When she returned a little before ten that night, she was a little apprehensive. Would someone be around to let her in? Stupid not to have asked for a key or a garage opener or something. She was delighted to find the garage open.

She did not expect the explosion that greeted her.

Jake stood in the garage, his expression a combination of relief and vexation. By the time she got out of the car, it had changed to outrage. "Where the hell have you been?" he demanded.

"At work."

"Work!"

She gasped. "You make it sound like... Look, it may be a four letter word, but it's not a forbidden one. It's an ordinary undertaking, indulged in by a majority of the population."

"But..." He hesitated, seeming more puzzled than angry. "I thought that while you...I guess I didn't expect my wife to work."

"Speaking of old-fashioned! Don't tell me you are one of those chauvinists threatened by a wife's career!"

His mouth quirked, and he almost grinned. "Oh, a career I could take. A chic little woman in an Armani suit, carrying a leather briefcase, and—"

"Oh, for goodness' sake," she broke in. She didn't need to be reminded that she was covered with crumbling plaster from Charlie's old walls, and it had been a long day. "Look, could we continue this conversation somewhere sitting down?"

"Good idea. Seems we have a good deal to say to each other. After you," he said, holding open the door to the house. "Are you hungry?" he asked, when she was seated in the little breakfast room.

"A little," she admitted.

"Well, it's a good thing I asked Sadie to serve a plate for you," he said as he got up and placed same in the microwave. "Even if I didn't know when or *if* you would be returning."

"What do you mean? You knew—"

"I didn't know a damn thing! I got up this morning all prepared to explain you to Sadie, and—"

"Who's Sadie?"

"My housekeeper. I told you the Hunts live here. Actually in that condo back of the garage. They manage everything."

"Oh. So why did you have to explain me to her?"

"Because she's been here since I was fifteen and is more of a mother hen than my mother. She sure as hell wouldn't understand any of this 'arranged' business!" The microwave buzzed as if to emphasize this statement. He retrieved the plate and set it before her.

"Oh, thank you." Smothered chicken, rice, gravy, and tiny green peas. It smelled so good.

"What do you want to drink?"

"Tea, please. Hot." That always helped settle her

stomach. "But not...would that be too much trouble."

"Not nearly as much trouble as explaining a missing bride," he declared as he prepared the tea. "I felt like a damn fool. I had Sadie convinced that I had, as we agreed, fallen passionately in love and married on impulse. So how do you suppose I felt when the blushing bride failed to appear? And not 'till almost midnight, when a very suspicious Sadie has retired and I'm going out of my mind! And that's another thing. Most folks work from nine to five, don't they? Why are you dragging in here at this hour?"

"Well, we wanted to finish the Carlsons' floor, so we didn't knock off 'till almost six. Charlie and I work on his house after-hours. Finally got rid of all that crumbling plaster, not all of it on me." She looked down at herself and chuckled. "Anyway, by the time I went to check on Jim it was almost nine. And...well, it does take some time to get from there to here, you know."

He was staring at her in amazement. "Just what kind of work do you do?"

"But I explained—"

"You didn't explain a damn thing!" He set the mug down so hard a little tea splashed out.

"But I told you that I had to take care of the business. I..." She stopped, thinking back to that doubtful time when she tried to find a way out of her dilemma. She had begged him to marry her, but had skimmed the details. She owed him that. So she told him about the bankruptcy, Crenshaw Construction, Jim's illness.

"I see," he said when she finished. "You're obligated. But, hell, we can fix that. We'll hire someone to take over until your stepfather is—"

"No." Her voice was sharp. "I promised not to touch a penny of your money and I intend to keep that promise!"

He stared at her. What kind of game was she playing now? She had agreed to marry Ben for a piddly two hundred, fifty thousand to save the damn business! He shrugged. "Well, call it a loan."

"No. That's how Jim got into trouble. Besides, I'm doing fine. And it's for me, too, don't you see? My means of support after...for me and the baby."

"Oh, for Christ sake, I told you—"

She reached over and touched his hand. "All I asked of you was a few months in this marriage. Nothing more. I mean to keep that promise."

"You made a few promises in Atlantic City yesterday, too."

She stared at him, puzzled. "Yes, but all that was pretend...just until..."

"What was it you said? If I'm going to live a lie, it'll have to be a big one. That goes for me, too. I told you I don't plan to look a trapped fool."

"What do you mean by that?"

"I mean you'll remain here long enough in the morning to meet the Hunts and take proper charge of your household. And you'll be here in the evening in time to accompany me to a seven o'clock dinner party which my friend, Scot Harding, is hosting to celebrate our recent nuptials.''

''Oh. Of course.'' It would cut a hole in her day, but she owed him that.

''And it will help if you could manage to look the happy bride you're supposed to be.''

''Sweetheart, meet Sadie and Ernie Hunt, who keep everything in order for me. And here she is at last,'' Jake said, pulling Judy close to him and nodding to the couple. ''She ducked out on us yesterday because she was concerned about her father who has just had heart surgery.''

''I am so glad to meet you, and sorry that I inconvenienced you. It was kind of you, Mrs. Hunt, to leave dinner for me. It was very good and I enjoyed it.'' Judy realized she was talking too fast and stopped, conscious of only one thing…Jake's arm around her. It didn't feel awkward at all. It felt comfortable. Supportive.

She needed his support. It was clear that she was the one being appraised. They were the permanent fixtures, she the intruder, and not a very welcome one. She could tell by the way they looked at her. Respectful, but aloof.

Ernie Hunt, a slightly built balding man, spoke first. ''We're glad to meet you, too, Mrs. Mason. We hope you'll be happy here, and we'll do our best to see that you are.''

"Yes, indeed we will. We've waited a long time for this, haven't we, Ernie?" Sadie asked her husband, but she was looking at Jake whose arm instinctively tightened around Judy. "Just let us know what you want or want changed. And what time would you like breakfast and dinner?"

"Ah, nothing. That is, I don't need..." Judy paused, trying to collect herself, trying to decipher the strange sensations ignited by Jake's touch. "I have a business in Richmond, you see, and I have to leave so early. I could fix toast and tea myself if I want," she sputtered. "And about dinner—"

"No dinner tonight, Sadie," Jake broke in, as if sensing her dilemma. "We're going out. And Judy's so busy, maybe we'd better play it by ear. Let you know each morning when we'll want dinner, huh, sweet?" He nuzzled her hair, distracting her so that she was barely able to nod.

Still acting the part of a loving husband, he escorted her to her car, and leaned in to remind her just before she drove off, "Try to get back before five. Give yourself time to dress."

"Oh. Yes. Is this a formal affair?" she asked, her mind reviewing her scanty wardrobe.

"Strictly casual. Well, not strictly. The other ladies...I'd like you to wear a dress."

"All right." She drove off, her skin still burning from his touch. She tried to focus on the day ahead. Stop at the Jones's to give an estimate on the new cabinets. Get in touch with Leo about that plumbing job. Charlie. Well, no work on his house tonight. She'd have to run by her house to pick up a dress...maybe that gold silk shirtwaist. Would Jake like it?

Darn it! What did she care whether he liked it or not! You're a one-night stand, kiddo, and this is a pretend marriage, and don't you forget it.

It was no use. He had barely touched her and she couldn't shake it off. If that was for the benefit of the servants, how would it be tonight with his best friends? Darn. She didn't know how much of this touchy touchy touch business she could stand.

Guess I look okay, she thought that night as she surveyed herself in her panel of mirrors. The gold dress seemed to highlight the gold in her hair which she had pinned up in a semi bun with a few curls cascading from it. Matching sandals, bare legs, and tiny gold hoops her only jewelry. Casual, but not too casual, she thought.

Just right, said Jake's admiring eyes, and she felt a little jolt of pride. Glad she had taken time for a manicure and pedicure. Glad, as he led her to the Porsche, that he seemed as anxious to avoid touching her as she was anxious not to be touched.

The Hardings lived in a different section of town, in a newer house, not quite as spacious as Jake's, but just as plush, she noted, as they drove through a well-manicured lawn to a Tudor English house. As soon as the wide double doors opened they were bombarded with confetti, bells, whistles and shouts from a hilarious crowd of well-wishers. Congratulations battled with recriminations.

"So you finally did it, you sneak!"

"Yeah, how come we got let out!"

"Don't knock it! He finally got hooked!"

"And no wonder!" Loud whistle. "If this is the little lady that did it!"

"Congratulations, buddy. But something's missing. Wasn't I supposed to be best man?"

There was lots of hugging and kissing, cocktails were served, with everyone talking at once even as introductions were made. She was surprised to discover that the "crowd" consisted of only three couples when they sat down to dinner and she was able to sort them out.

Scot Harding, the handsome dark-haired man who was host, helped her. "If he—" pointing to Jake "—gives you any trouble, just call on me. I've been keeping him straight since kindergarten. And don't let Lisa get to you. She third degrees any woman who comes near Jake."

"Lisa?"

"My wife." He gestured toward the other end of the table at the pretty woman with the dimples and frosted hair. "She thinks she's Jake's personal protector and... Hey, how'd she miss you? Wow! You guys really put one over on us. But I forgive you. I can tell just by looking that you're the best thing that's happened to him."

During such chatter she learned about the other two

couples. Hal Stanford, an Afro-American, was one of the vice presidents in the same insurance company with Scot. "That's Doris, his wife, sitting next to Jake."

"And I'm Senator Dobbs." The short stocky man on her left nodded with exaggerated pomposity. "I am particularly interested in your political persuasions and I—"

"Shut up, Al!" Jake, across the table cut in. "Pay him no mind, Judy. He's a two-bit politician who's only here because he's married to my cousin, Ada, over there."

It was through such jesting that she learned she was with the "in" crowd, couples so close they could cap on each other. Couples. Jake was part of the group. Who was the other part of his couple? The mysterious Mel whom everyone had carefully avoided mentioning? Judy felt a stab of pure jealousy. This was a fun group. She wished she was really a part of it.

"So, Jake," Scot said. "Do we meet in the morning or does your bride keep you locked in?"

Jake looked at Judy. "Scot and I have a golf thing on Saturday mornings…that is, when we're both in place. You don't mind, do you, sweetheart?"

"Of course not," Judy said, flushing from the "sweetheart." He said it as if—

"Good," Scot said. "This'll be the first time since Ben Cruz's wedding. Did he get off okay?"

Ben. Judy sat up. This was the first time his name

had been mentioned. He was part of this "in" group, wasn't he? Jake's best friend.

"Who's Ben Cruz?" Al asked.

"Oh, he's one of Jake's pet charities," Scot answered. "Since college. Ben hung around the school, doing odd jobs, such as waiting table at the frat house. One night he pushed Jake out of the way of a car that plowed into the building, and got himself a bankroll for life. When the roll gets low he contacts Jake, who has staked him for most anything from a chicken farm to a pizza parlor."

Not the way Ben told it, Judy thought. She looked straight at Jake, her eyes flashing the message, You didn't tell me! He tore his eyes from hers, and cut into his prime rib.

"Clever fellow." The senator took a swallow of wine. "He knew whom to save. Couldn't have picked a bigger sucker!"

"Right," Scot said. "Do you know why he went on the wild rafting trip in Bolivia? Course he loves skirting with danger and the poor little rich guy has nothing else to do, unlike us nine-to-fivers!"

"Leave Jake alone," Lisa called. "He can go rafting when and wherever he chooses!"

"Right. I'm just telling you why he went on this particular one. These two guys, not yet thirty, yearned to start their own company, offering rafting tours to the wildest regions on earth. What do you think? They needed a stake."

"And the lucky so-and-so's ran into the give-away

king!'' Hal Stanford said, amid a series of chuckles from the group.

"You got it. And they got it, didn't they, Jake? Two guys, still in their twenties who don't know beans about—''

"Wrong. They know their business. I went on the trip, remember? And it's a damn good business. Would you rather have them out selling drugs or something?''

"Okay, buddy. Maybe it'll work out. Tell them I've got a good insurance package for them. They sure as hell will need it. And what about Ben? Did he marry an heiress and get off your hands? Where is he now?''

"He got off, and I'm not sure where he is,'' Jake said, and then, as if in an effort to change the subject, "I'm too busy trying to keep up with a working wife.''

"A working wife!'' Adam, the senator's wife exclaimed. "You're a career woman?''

"Yes, I'm a contractor,'' Judy said, evoking a series of questions and comments on the rather unusual occupation for a woman.

"My wife is a career woman,'' Scot said when the comments dwindled.

"Oh?'' Judy was surprised. "You work?''

Lisa's dimples danced as she stuck out her tongue at her husband. "Yes, in the home.''

"Marriage is her career. She informed me before she offered herself in matrimony that it is the grandest, most rewarding profession on earth, right up there next to prostitution, didn't you, sweet?''

With roars of laughter, the teasing now focused on Lisa, who was supported by Stanford's wife, who declared that it was certainly the hardest job on earth.

If marriage was her career, she was making quite a success of it, Judy decided. She and Scot seemed so happy, so attuned to each other. So much in love, she thought as the group retreated to the living room for coffee, and Lisa nestled close to her husband who couldn't seem to keep his hands off her.

They look ready for us to clear out, she thought, and was unprepared when Lisa sat up and dropped the bomb. "All right, you two. Tell us. All of it. Where you two met. How the romance developed. We want the whole thing!''

Judy's startled gaze flew across the room to meet Jake's blank look. Another detail they hadn't planned.

Her mind groped. "Er...sailing!'' she gasped.

"Right!'' Jake's face cleared and he grinned.

"I was sitting on the deck of the *Bluebird*, minding my own business, when I spotted this gal, pardon me...female person in quite a predicament. She was obviously green about sailing, and was having a deal of trouble trying to launch a little boat which she...she...'' He hesitated, and Judy who had been staring at him in amazement, realized he was asking for help.

"I had rented it,'' she said quickly. "The man told

me anybody could handle it, so I thought of course I could.''

Jake tapped his head significantly. ''A bit green about other things to.''

''I am not!'' She made a face at her husband. She was enjoying this. ''I just don't think the man gave me enough instructions.''

''You see?'' Jake spread his hands. ''Under the circumstances...''

''Aha!'' Scot broke in. ''Captain Mason to the rescue! Being the knight in shining armor, or perhaps it was the sight of all that golden hair.''

''Nope.'' Jake shook his head. ''The sight of that round bottom in those blue shorts.''

''Okay, I'll buy that,'' Stanford said. ''And then what?''

''Well, I thought she should try a real boat...like the *Bluebird*.'' He didn't say much more, but what he said sounded so much like the real days on the *Bluebird* that Judy found herself dabbing surreptitiously at her eyes with her napkin.

''You managed that part about our meeting very well,'' she told him as they drove home.

He shrugged. ''Necessity is the mother of invention, my dear.''

''We've been doing a lot of inventing lately, haven't we?'' she said, trying to keep the bitterness out of her voice. ''We're getting to be as big liars as Ben Cruz.''

He shot her a quick glance, but said nothing.

"You didn't even tell me," she persisted.

"What was the point? It was after the fact. Anyway, you were going to marry the guy, in love and all that. I'm not into bursting bubbles."

"But even afterward. When I told you I didn't love him, that it wa—"

"Okay, okay!" he broke in. He didn't want to hear again that it was the money. "Now you know. Can't we just drop it? You're a hell of a lot better off without him, and I'm—" He broke off, but she heard it anyway... "I'm stuck with you!"

CHAPTER TEN

HE REALLY didn't mind that his wife worked. To tell the truth, he envied her. She got up early each morning, with somewhere to go. People waiting for her. Something needing to be done.

Nobody cared if he slept in all day. He wasn't needed anywhere. Not even at any of his various board meetings unless someone was trying to get some issue through and needed his vote.

It must feel good to be needed.

Each morning when he heard the shower in her bath, he pictured her under the streaming water, her hair clinging to her skin. Like it had that night. No, she must wrap it in a towel, he decided. It was certainly dry, and tied on top of her head, the two mornings he arranged to meet her as she came out of her room.

"Coffee?" he had asked.

"Thanks, but I'd better not. I want to beat the traffic."

His eyes focused on her bottom as she hurried away. Damn but she looked cute in those tight jeans. He wondered how long... When did babies begin to show? He went back into his room to watch, as was his habit, when the little Volkswagen pulled out of the garage and turned down the driveway.

She ought to have something better than that rattle-trap to beat the traffic, he thought that stormy morning her car pulled out of the garage and stopped. She got out, looked down at the rear left tire. She stamped a foot, then vent her rage on the car, pounding with her fists, unmindful of the pouring rain. She looked so funny, he grinned. At least she had on a raincoat, and a rain hat pulled low over her head.

He watched her pull open the trunk and take out...a jack?

A flat tire? And she intended to fix it herself? Jesus! He hurriedly pulled on some pants and rushed down-stairs. He had to get to the fool woman before she started working with that jack.

When he reached her, however, she had dropped the jack, and was leaning against the car, being very very sick. He felt sick himself, just watching her. He pulled her back against him, his hand gently holding her stomach, as if to ease the eruptions.

It was some time before it was over, and she straightened. "Thank you. I'm sorry. I made such a mess. I never know when. I'm sorry."

"No reason to be sorry. It's not your fault."

She had pulled from him and was looking at her watch. "It's late. I have to get cleaned up. Do you think...that is, would Ernie mind fixing this tire for me? I need to—"

"You need to do lots of things," he said, picking her up.

"Wait. This isn't necessary. I feel fine now. I can manage."

He paid no attention to her protests as he carried her through the house and into her bedroom, dripping water everywhere.

"You are a fool," he said as he began to strip off her clothes. "Standing out there in the middle of a storm."

"Me! I had on a raincoat. Look at you."

"Never mind about me." He might be bare-footed and dripping wet, but he wasn't pregnant.

"Stop it! There's no need to take off all my clothes."

"Oh, shut up!" he said, throwing aside her boots and unzipping her jeans. "This won't be the first time I've seen you naked, will it!"

"Listen to me! I've got to go. Charlie—"

"You're not going anywhere, Charlie or no Charlie." Having removed the last of her clothes, he looked around for a gown. Not seeing one, he pulled back the blankets and dumped her into the bed as she was.

She struggled to get up. "Look, I told you. I have to go. Charlie needs me to—"

"You're not going anywhere." She might be smarter. And needed. But he was bigger.

She wanted to slap him. Beg him, make him understand. But she was so tired. The bed felt so good.

If she could just lie here a few minutes. The vomiting took so much out of her. He had held her. Made her feel not so alone.

"Can I get you something? Dry toast? Tea?"

She nodded. "Thank you." That always helped. Then she could—

"Only if you promise not to move."

She blinked. He was kind. She touched his arm. "I know you mean well. But, truly, I am all right. And there's so much to be done. Charlie needs the specs on that other house. And Jim is home now, you see. I didn't get over there yesterday and— Oh, dear, what about my flat tire!"

"Okay. You promise to stay here, and we'll figure out how to take care of all that when I get back. Deal?"

She nodded. She couldn't go anywhere on a flat anyway.

Over toast and tea, more promises were made. She would stay put, and he would go into Richmond, take Charlie the specs, and go by the house to check on Jim.

"Don't tell them I'm sick. Well, maybe a virus or something," she said. "I don't want to tell them about the child until I have to. And be sure to tell Jim that things are going well, whether you think so or not."

He promised, but she was still anxious when he left. She didn't want him to go. She liked to look after things herself.

But the electrician would be waiting for Charlie to

bring those specs. And Jim needed constant reassurance.

Somebody had to go.

She was tired. It felt good. To just lie here. To sleep.

It was still raining when, following her directions, he reached Charlie's house. He mounted the steps, pressed a doorbell, and looked around the front porch which, judging by the spots of new lumber, had undergone some improvement. Probably scheduled for a paint job that would pull it all together.

The door was opened by a tall muscular man. "Charlie?" Jake asked.

"Sure thing. What can I do for you?"

"I'm Judy's husband. She asked me to bring these," Jake said, handing over the specs.

"Thank you. Where's Judy? I wondered…is something wrong? Oh, come in," he said, stepping back.

He walked into a room where the man was obviously in the process of laying Sheetrock. He remembered Judy's "We got all that crumbling plaster off Charlie's walls."

He joined Charlie and his wife for a cup of coffee, assured them that Judy was okay, probably just a one-day virus, admired the baby, and asked to accompany Charlie on his rounds. "Promised Judy I'd give her dad a full report."

After delivering the specs to the electrician, Charlie expanded his rounds so that Jake could view the whole picture. He took him by the house that the electrician was rewiring. "Judy's got a thing about this new indirect lighting, and it sure does brighten up these old houses." They stopped by to check on Leo, who was installing a Jacuzzi. He even took him by the Jacksons' to proudly show off the finished attic. "Judy and I did this one all by ourselves."

Jake tried to imagine Judy at work here in this big room, now littered with toys. Working with hammer and saw to perfect the built-in cabinets and the sloping ceilings which somehow reminded him of the *Bluebird*. He was caught by the map-of-the-world wallpaper, the bright cheerful look of the place, even on this dreary day with the rain pounding against the windowpane. The new indirect lighting?

Back at the East End, Charlie pointed out a couple of the dilapidated houses and told about their plans.

It was exciting, Jake thought, as he drove away. So many projects going at once. Building, improving, putting people to work. No wonder she was eager to get up in the middle of the night and rush over here. Where something was happening, and she was the pilot!

An old familiar feeling stirred within him. That feeling of being outside, looking in, while someone else did the work, put across an idea.

She wasn't playing any game. She meant it when she said she wanted no part of his money. No part of his do-nothing world. No part of him.

And their child was an impediment that had stopped her in her tracks. Trapped her.

She was trying to keep going. He thought of her this morning, standing in the rain. Furious. Frustrated. And uncontrollably sick.

Poor kid.

Well, darn it, he could make it easier for her, couldn't he! Whether she wanted him to or not! She was an independent little cuss!

He gave Jim Taylor a glowing report, and assured them that Judy's "virus" would only last a couple of days. Alicia persuaded him to stay for lunch, during which he wondered how such a silly woman managed to produce a daughter like Judy.

He liked Jim Taylor. A straightforward man, weak, but anxious to get back to work, to "take some of that load off Judy." Yes, he agreed, it was a long day for her. Better to come in after, rather than before, the rush hour.

"And return before the evening rush," Jake said. "I don't mind my wife working, but I do like to see her occasionally," he added with all the eagerness of a loving husband.

"Of course. Of course," Jim agreed. "Sets up the right routine for me when I take over. The doctors say I'll have to take it easy for a while."

Jake smiled. That was all he needed.

Judy wondered if Jake told Sadie she was pregnant. Something had changed her attitude. She fussed over

Judy when she brought up her breakfast and lunch trays, telling her to, "eat slowly and take a sip of this ginger ale every now and then. It will settle your stomach." She hung up Judy's clothes and straightened the room, chatting cheerfully as she did so, asking what would she like for dinner. Making Judy feel, for the first time, a part of the household.

After lunch, Judy took a long nap, awoke feeling rested, refreshed. By the time Jake returned, she had showered and donned the lounging pajamas that had been part of her trousseau.

"I'm fine now," she said when he came up to check on her. "I told you I always am once that stupid heaving is over. But, okay...I did enjoy the rest."

"Good."

"But now I don't know what to do with myself." She had finished all the paperwork for the business, and there wasn't a thing to read in the room. Nothing but soap operas on TV. "I feel funny just goofing off."

"I know the feeling." Something in the way he said it made her sad. Then he smiled. "But it's raining. A goofing off day. Come on down to the den, there's plenty to read down there."

As they went downstairs, she bombarded him with questions. "Was everything going all right? Did Charlie get those specs to Todd? Did you get to see Jim?"

"Yes, yes, and yes." He grinned and began to sing in a surprisingly good baritone. "'Without your pulling it, the tide comes in. Without your twirling it, the earth can spin. Without you—'''

"Oh, stop it!" she cried, laughing. "I know I'm not indispensable. But there's so much to be done and so few of us. I'll have to go in tomorrow. Oh! Did you ask Ernie about my tire?"

"Took care of it," he said, not looking at her as he opened the door to the den. "Plenty of magazines in that rack. Or, if you prefer a book—"

"Oh, no! I don't dare start on a book. No telling when I'll have another day like this or any time to lollygag."

"Oh, I don't know. Jim thinks you might be overdoing it," he said, joining her on the sofa.

The magazine remained unopened in her lap. "You mean, working too hard? That doesn't bother me."

"Overdoing your role. And that bothers him."

"Did he say that?" She looked anxious. Just where he wanted her. Anything to please Jim, he thought. Okay, he'd lay it on thick.

"Yep. Says you're making things hard for him."

"Hard? How so?"

"Well, seems the doctors have ordered that when he does go back to work, he'd have to take it easy. He was rather hoping you'd build up a large enough crew, so that all he would need to do was oversee."

"Well, we are hiring more workers. And I'd be there to help."

"You're going to be incapacitated for a while yourself. Remember?"

"That's right," she said, looking frustrated and slightly disgusted. "Probably about the time he returns."

"Jim said it might be good if you set up the procedure now. You handle drawings, estimates, paperwork, things like that. Charlie could oversee the actual work. And he'd like you to cut your hours. Come in later in the morning, around ten. Knock off sooner. So when he gets back, the routine is all set. See?"

"I guess that does make sense. Funny he never said anything to me about that."

"The man's just getting back on his feet, Judy. This is the first time he's had to think about it."

And you stopped to listen, she thought. Suddenly she felt a surge of gratitude. He had driven into Richmond to take the papers to Charlie, stopped to really listen to Jim. Held her this morning, so tenderly... "It was so kind of you to go in today, Jake. I really appreciate..." She touched his hand, and, jolted by the sensations spinning through her, drew quickly back. "Your taking all this time with Jim. And me," she muttered, feeling muddled. Crazy. Just touching him. She'd have to remember not to.

He was staring at her, and she felt she ought to say something more. "I guess he does make sense," she repeated. "It would be easier on me, too, right now."

"Yeah. Might be." He picked up a deck of cards. "How about a game of gin?"

It did seem funny to sit down to a proper meal a little before nine the next morning. Judy was surprised that the delicious breakfast Sadie had prepared stayed down. Surprised that Jake joined her. It was pleasant.

"Have a nice day," she told him as she left the table and went to the garage to get into her Volkswagen.

It wasn't there.

In its place stood a very new shiny black Cherokee Jeep. Beautiful. Neat.

Not hers.

Instinctively she turned. Yes, he had followed her. "Where's my car?" she demanded. "You told me Ernie had fixed the tire."

He shook his head. "I told you I took care of it."

"Took care! Did you dump—"

"Don't be ridiculous. I wouldn't dump anything of yours. It's stored away and can be picked up at any time."

"Well, I want it picked up now."

"Why?"

"Because…" It was hers. The only thing of any value that she had brought with her. "I need it," she finished.

"Don't you like the substitute?" He walked around the Jeep, kicked at a tire.

She sighed. It was a sturdy good-looking vehicle. "I like it. But I think we should stick to our agreements. I promised not to take anything from you."

"I remind you again of promises, sincere or not, made in Atlantic City. To me."

"I'm keeping those promises. I'm living here. I'm—"

"Driving down the freeway each morning in a car that looks like it's about to fall apart. It's not safe."

"It hasn't fallen apart."

"And it doesn't look professional."

"Not pro...? What do you mean by that?"

"I mean I went to a lot of damn trouble to select the right model, so you'd look like the professional contractor you are."

She stared at him. He was serious. Yesterday, in that storm, he'd gone to Richmond, taken care of her business, talked to Jim. Then he'd gone shopping for a car. Not just any car. The right car. For her.

And she was rewarding him with a show of stupid irrational petty pride! Her shame combined with the sudden rush of tenderness, and she reached out to touch him. "Oh, Jake, I'm sorry." She stepped back, resisting the impulse to throw her arms around him. "Forgive me. I'm being very silly. I don't mean to be ungrateful." She ran her tongue over her lip, and tried to explain, to herself as well as to him. "It's just that it was such a surprise. Overwhelming. I've never owned anything like it. No. Wait. I don't want to own it. Couldn't we just call it a loaner until after..." She trailed off, not wanting to finish the thought.

"Call it anything you like. Only drive it. It's safer and better than what you had."

After that day, tensions eased and their lives, separate and together, continued on a pretty even keel. The shorter hours, and the lighter load, made Judy's work-day much easier. She returned to find a delicious dinner and a pleasant household waiting. Surprisingly, Jake usually joined her for dinner. He was sometimes out of town, but not nearly as often as she had expected.

It was an early pretty rough winter, and after dinner, they often lingered by the fire in the den.

"Want to try it?" he asked one evening, gesturing toward the alcove nearest the fire where a chess table was always set with the beautiful silver chess pieces inherited, he said, from his grandfather.

"Me?" she gasped. "I don't know beans about that game. It's always looked too complicated for me."

"Coward! Come on. I'll teach you."

It was a difficult game, but absolutely fascinating, and she thoroughly enjoyed the hours spent at that little table.

Who had spent these hours with him before? she wondered. Played chess with him? Been his partner when the clan got together?

They often got together, at each other's houses, or sometimes at the club. They had welcomed her. Lisa, Scot's wife, and Doris, Hal Stanford's wife, often included her in their strictly women's gatherings, lunch, shopping, or whatever. She liked them, and evidently they liked her, for they soon began to confide in her. Doris was an attorney who had given up her practice to rear her two boys. She had planned to go back when her two boys were past the baby-sitting years. "Then," Doris said, "oops, along came my toddler, Ann Marie."

"She's prettier and more cuddly than a stuffy old law office," Lisa declared. "If you don't want her, I'll take her."

"No way! Leave my baby alone!" Doris laughed. "Get your own."

"I'm trying. I'm trying," Lisa said, and confided that she was longing for a child. But after a year and a half of marriage, she was not yet pregnant.

Ironic, Judy thought, as the intimate discussion continued. She remembered an old saying…"Them that has, gets." That was Doris all right. And Lisa…"Those who want, can't."

While I…well, I certainly didn't want a child, and I wasn't trying. But…in just one night. If they only knew. How that one night has changed my whole life.

However, no matter how intimate the conversation, there was one subject never touched. They had welcomed her into the group as if she had always belonged, and no matter how much they teased, never once mentioned another woman in connection with Jake, not even the mysterious Mel. And this abstention made Judy all the more curious.

She finally got up enough courage to question Lisa. "You do so many things together. As couples, I mean. I keep wondering, who was Jake's partner before me?"

"Before you?" Lisa looked puzzled. "It seems to

me, first one, then another. Nobody lasted very long. Of course, you'll have to remember, I've only been part of the group about a year myself. But Scot says it was always that way with Jake. Says he's always been wary about getting too close to anyone. 'Course there were plenty trying to get close to him.''

"Yes, I can understand that. A bachelor, handsome, eligible—''

"Rich?'' Lisa supplied, laughing.

"Well, yes. All that. And I wonder...there must have been someone before me.''

"There was. Me.''

"You!'' Judy stared at her in amazement. She had never seen a couple as much in love as Scot and Lisa. And they both were like family to Jake.

Lisa was nodding and grinning. "Isn't that crazy? But he had asked me and I was going to marry him because he was so rich. But I couldn't because I didn't love him. And, truthfully, he didn't love me, either. We often laugh about it now. And then...'' Lisa bent forward confidentially. "It was Jake who told me I was in love with Scot. I didn't know it, and Scot didn't know it. But Jake did. Jake is very perceptive. And such a sweet guy. I'm glad he's married to you, Judy. He deserves someone who really loves him. And you do. I can see it in your eyes every time you look at him.''

Judy's breath caught. Did it show? She had thought that if she didn't touch him...

She must be more careful.

CHAPTER ELEVEN

IT WAS just a slight thud in the pit of her stomach, so light as to be barely noticeable. But Judy felt it. It shook her to the roots.

Something inside her was alive and kicking.

Awesome!

Her hands closed over her stomach, instinctively holding and protecting this little thing that was so vibrantly alive. There! There it was again. A baby...living and growing.

A boy? With sea blue eyes that would squint in the sun?

"Couldn't you, Judy?"

"What?" Judy gave Doris Stanford a blank look. She had forgotten where she was. Sitting in the club lounge with Lisa and Doris while they waited for the men to finish their racquetball game and join them for lunch.

"Couldn't you, Judy?" Doris repeated as if trying to nudge her awake. "I don't mean from you personally. Jake used his muscle as board chair of M & S, and presto, they donated two television sets."

Lisa grunted. "And he'd have given you a bundle worth more if you'd asked for cash. Mary is right," she said, quoting as she often did from the woman who had raised her. "She says all these rich people waste time and energy with auctions and charity balls. If they'd just make a donation instead—"

"Oh, do be quiet, Lisa. This auction has been held by the foundation every fall for the past fifteen years. I just happen to be on the fund-raising committee, and I just happen to be obligated to secure items for the auction sufficient to meet our goal. Besides the busywork, it's fun and we, as well as you, really enjoy the event."

"Touché!" Lisa agreed. "I stand corrected. Carry on."

"Judy, I mean Crenshaw Construction. It'll be well advertised, and of course, a tax deduction. See?"

"Yes. Well, okay. I'll think of something," Judy said, back on track with the conversation now. What would be a suitable contribution from a contracting firm? A well-outfitted toolbox? She gave a wry smile. As if any of the wealthy people attending the auction would have any use for a toolbox! Maybe Lisa's Mary was right!

"Well, ladies, are you ready for lunch?" Jake's voice was husky as it always was right after his shower. His hair was damp and clinging.

Judy's breath caught, and all thought of auctions went out of her head. She was hardly aware of the cheerful banter that continued as the group filed into the dining room. She was envisioning a tiny baby girl with straw-colored sun-bleached hair.

"Bring us a bottle of your best champagne," Jake

said to the waiter who nodded and hurried off. "This calls for a celebration, ladies."

"What does?" Doris asked.

"Nothing momentous," Scot said. "Just his usual luck."

"Did you lose, too?" somebody asked Hal.

"Me? Oh, I just worked out. I know better than to match up against a pro," he answered, and the usual banter began. Of course Jake won. He was a pro at play because play was all he did.

That irritated Judy. Jake was good at sports because...well, he was just good! She remembered how careful and precise he was at handling the *Bluebird*. She could see his strong hands gripping the oars that night, holding the little skiff against the wind and the pounding waves.

Hands that had caressed her so tenderly that night. She felt the thud again, and one hand flew to her stomach...holding, caressing. She felt herself flush, quickly drew her hand away, glanced across the table at Jake. She watched him taste the champagne, smile, and give the waiter an okay sign. Scot and Hal were still doing the privileged rich playboy bit. She knew they were teasing, but somehow, this morning it irritated her. Why didn't Jake defend himself instead of just sitting there, grinning?

In the middle of lunch the waiter brought a note to Jake.

He read it, excused himself, saying he had to make a call. "Be right back."

Hal watched him leave then glanced at Scot. "Bet it's that merger caper."

Scot nodded. "Sure. I agree, and I bet he'll stop it."

"Right, I believe he will."

"Easy," Scot said. "Just like he breezed through that MBA at Harvard."

"Funny he's always shunned the desk and corporate routine," Hal mused.

"But he's uncanny at freelance investment and boardsmanship."

By this time Judy's ears were on fire. What was with this merger thing? She was glad to hear Lisa ask, "What's going on? Would you please let us in on it? What's going on?"

Scot said, "It's no secret now. Jake just upset a well-orchestrated merger. M & S, Incorporated, would gobble Atkins Communication Service, and investors' dividends would soar."

"That's good, isn't it?" Doris asked.

Hal pointed a finger at Judy. "Your man didn't think so. Since it would reduce staff by twenty thousand, consequently putting those people out on the streets."

"Oh, that would be bad," Judy said. "Too many companies are doing just that."

"Exactly what Jake thought," Hal said. "He locked horns with the pro merger crowd who had orchestrated the coup. He argued that the market price of both Mason and Sellers and Atkins would fall. Not increase. He believed it was no longer profitable for investors to support deals that displaced people. Earnings. At the end of his discourse, we've been told, he simply asked, 'What happens when the twenty-five thousand wage earners stop buying our products and services?' There were no good answers, and both boards demurred. They are back at the drawing board. Jake has been asked to chair the task force.''

"No easy task,'' Scot said. "He'll not have time to play for a while.''

But he'll be in there pitching for the workers, Judy thought with a glow of pride. Her hand again closed protectively over her stomach. Someone alive in there. She wanted him—her?—to grow up to be as smart and as caring as his father.

Jake returned, concern on his face. "Sorry, folks. Judy, we'll have to leave. I need to be in New York. Like now.''

Judy was naturally small, and the full dresses and oversized sweaters helped. But, by the middle of November she could no longer conceal the little mound that was slowly but surely beginning to appear.

"And you never said one word,'' Doris cried, and, observing her critically, added, "You must be three, maybe four months along.''

"About,'' Judy said, wondering why she was being evasive. At worst, even if they counted, it would appear that she had gotten pregnant on her wedding night.

"Why all the secrecy?" Lisa cried. "If it were me, I'd have been shouting from the roof... Hear ye, hear ye... Come one, come all. Why didn't you let us in on it?"

"Guess I was a little ashamed...getting pregnant so early," Judy admitted. At least that was the truth.

"Well, it's out now. We'll have to go shopping for maternity clothes," Lisa said. "I'll help you. Maybe I'll buy one for myself. It might be catching."

"That's not the way you catch it!" Doris chortled.

"Oh, hush, Miss Smarty. I know how to catch it. Scot says that's the fun part! And just because you're Old Mother Hubbard herself—"

"Three children do not a Mother Hubbard make! And wait. I'm coming with you. I'm an expert on maternity clothes."

Doris, the expert, pointed out the best features of each dress, and Lisa really did buy one for herself. "Just for good luck," she said.

They had such a good time shopping that Judy wondered why she had been so reluctant to share her secret. They were so excited about the pregnancy, so interested, and delighted. When they stopped for a light supper after shopping, the talk was all about pregnancy and what to do when the baby arrived. Judy began to absorb the excitement, the anticipation and joy of being with child.

She had reached home, and was taking her packages from the Jeep when Jake's Porsche pulled in beside her. He was out in an instant to help her unload. "Looks like you've been shopping."

"Absolutely necessary. I was coming out of my clothes."

"I see." Jake grinned as he tried to handle all the packages and dropped one. "This looks like you won't be running out of something to wear."

"Lisa and Doris. I really didn't need all this but they… Here, I'll get it." She stooped with some difficulty to pick up the box he had dropped, retrieved the rest of the parcels and followed him in. "They made me. Said I should avoid wearing the same thing over and over again. And they've got me outfitted for every occasion, working clothes to cocktail dresses."

"Sounds like a good plan. Do I get a showing?" he asked, turning to her.

"Oh." She stopped to avoid bumping into him, and dropped another bundle. "Would you like to see them?" She wanted to show off what she had bought. To him.

"Sure. Why not? Leave that. I'll get it. And come on into the den. I'll build up the fire and we'll have a fashion show."

"No. Take these up to my room. We don't need to be hauling all this stuff all over the place."

"Okay," he agreed. "I'll build up the fire in your room."

Maybe she should have settled for the den, she thought as she mounted the stairs. The bedroom was more…intimate? Not really, she argued with herself, as she directed him to place his bundles in her dressing room. There wouldn't have been any changing area in the den.

She went into the dressing room, arranging the dresses and pants on racks in the tiny closet. Doris and Lisa had been thorough, she thought. They had even selected low-heeled shoes for her comfort as well as to complement the outfits. Beautiful things. She hadn't known maternity clothes could be so lovely. She was anxious to show them off to Jake. She touched the silk lavender sheath, her favorite. Should that be first? No, she decided to save the best for last, and start with the work clothes.

"Especially for the working mother to be," she called gaily as she stepped from the dressing room. "These kelly green wool pants..." She stopped, unable to utter another word. The light from the lamps and the crackling fire made a soft glow, but it was like a bulwark against the outside winter dark, enveloping in a warmth, so pleasant, so cozy that... Why had she never lit the logs that were always there? Not there long enough or too tired when she was? Or because there was no Jake, as there was now, reclining on the lounge, sipping a martini, smiling that smile. Looking at her with those eyes. Her heart gave a little leap.

"Okay, okay. Come on with the spiel! Designed for the working mother to be..." he prompted.

She made a valiant effort to control her thoughts, concentrate on her words. "Kelly green wool pants," she repeated, making a professional model's turn as she continued, "with matching cashmere sweater, cleverly designed to conceal a bulging middle."

Jake put down his drink and clapped. "Very cleverly designed. We'll take it, madam."

He always made things so easy and comfortable, she thought as she made a smart exit.

After that it was easy. As much fun as shopping had been. More. She paraded and turned, professionally exhibiting each outfit. He admired, complemented, approved each one.

When at last she reached for the lavender cocktail dress, she felt sad that it was almost over. She had liked displaying her clothes. Liked his watching her. She slipped the soft dress over her head and gazed at herself in the mirror. It could have been a little fuller, she thought. The little mound in her middle was almost visible. But she had liked the way it clung to her and the slits on each side that complimented her legs which, thankfully, were holding their own. Even a pregnant woman could look sexy sometimes, couldn't she!

When she stood before him, Jake didn't smile or clap his hands. He put his drink down, stood up, and just looked at her. A look as intimate as his touch. A look that made her head spin and set her body on fire.

She couldn't move. She was held captive by those sea blue eyes that scanned every inch of her, that reached inside her, and made her come alive. Instinctively her hand covered her middle.

"Let me," he said, moving toward her and slipping his hand under hers. "Fathers-to-be have some rights," he said as he drew her to him and began to gently massage the little mound that had become part of her.

She couldn't have stopped him any more than she could have stopped breathing. No more than she could have stopped the delicious warmth stealing through her. A deep desire pulsing through her, begging to be fulfilled.

More compelling than the intoxicating passion was the tenderness. The gentleness of his touch. His caring.

They were married, weren't they?

She was carrying his child, wasn't she?

And she could no more have stopped the erotic yearning surging through her than she could have stopped the earth from turning. She wrapped her arms around him as he carried her to bed.

CHAPTER TWELVE

THE next morning, Judy slept late. When something, the rain beating against the windows, or the charred log that fell from the grate, tried to nudge her awake, she resisted. She kept her eyes shut tight, refusing to let go of the dream. His gentle caring touch, the whispered words of love. The ecstasy of fulfillment. The joy.

The rain beat harder against the windowpane. She smiled. It wasn't a dream! Last night... His arms around her, his love, had been for real.

She stirred contentedly, reaching for his warmth. Her eyes flew open. He wasn't there.

She sat up, missing him, but undisturbed. She listened for his shower, or perhaps he was downstairs making coffee. The Hunts took weekends off. It will be nice to spend this whole Sunday alone with him. Eager to join him, she got up to get her robe.

The note was on her closet mirror, where she couldn't miss it. "Good morning, love. You are so beautiful, so incredibly lovable, so special to me. I hate to leave you, this morning of all mornings. But business calls...in New York. You, my sexy little temptress, bewitched me out of leaving last night. I'm glad I didn't. Last night was incredible. Compatible, wouldn't you say? We need to talk. Keep sweet 'till I return, probably Tuesday. J.''

She hugged the note to her. "Good morning, love." She was his love. She was special for him. She memorized the words, rehearsed the pleasures of the night, and reveled in a contentment that was new to her. No. Not just contented. She was deliriously happy. Her precariously tilting world had suddenly righted itself. He loved her. She knew from his whispered words, his tender lovemaking. And she loved him, more than she ever thought she could love anyone.

She picked up the lavender dress that had been cast to the floor, held it against her cheek. You started it, you sexy thing! Thank you, thank you, thank you, she muttered as she hung it in the closet.

She practically danced downstairs and into the kitchen. She filled the coffeepot with cold water, reached into the cupboard for the coffee beans. Stopped. Looked around, overwhelmed by the thought. This was her kitchen. This was home. She lived here with a husband who loved her. He had grown up in this house. Their child would grow up here. She touched the counter, feeling a surge of sweet possessiveness. She would care for this house. Her child. And Jake. They would be happy.

The phone rang, startling her. She took it from the wall.

Lisa. "Did you show the outfits to Jake?"

"Yes."

"Did he love them? Oh, I know he did. They were just darling on you. Especially that lavender. What did he say?"

That I was his love, that I was special. "That...that he liked it...all of them." What he said about the clothes had gone completely out of her mind.

"I didn't dare show mine to Scot. He'd get the idea I was pregnant and be disappointed when he found I wasn't. Oh, Judy, I wish...I'm going to touch that dress every day and make a wish."

"And I'm going to wish for you, Lisa."

They talked awhile longer about inconsequential things, and when they hung up, Judy felt another surge of contentment. She was really a part of the group now, a normal happily married wife just like Lisa and Doris. The thought seemed to be confirmed by a kick from the baby, and she laughed. "Okay, I'm starving, too," she said, as she reached into the fridge for eggs and bacon.

She had wanted to spend this Sunday with Jake, but it was almost as nice just thinking about him. Coffee and bacon, my favorite morning smells, she had told him that first day on the *Bluebird*, when he had fixed breakfast for her.

The rain had not let up, and it was a cold dreary day outside. But Judy did not feel dreary, nor alone, as she sat at breakfast, the Sunday paper spread before her.

The phone rang.

Probably Doris, Judy thought as she went to pick it up. Or, she thrilled at the thought, maybe Jake.

It was neither Doris nor Jake. It was a low, rather musical feminine voice she had never heard before. It asked for Jake. "Is he still there?"

"Here?" She felt a little confused, but managed, "No, he isn't."

"He's left for New York?"

Probably someone calling about his meeting, Judy thought. "He left this morning. He should be—"

"This morning! Darn! He was supposed to be here last night."

She had to ask. "Who's calling please? Can I give him a message?"

"Oh, this is Mel. Who are you? Oh, never mind. No message. I'll see him when he gets here. Thanks."

Judy's hand tightened on the phone as the line went dead.

Mel. As if it were yesterday, she saw the blue Armani shorts and top she had taken from a drawer in the *Bluebird*. Saw the slacks and sundresses that lined the closet. Sandals and sport shoes for a long slender foot.

The robe she had wrapped herself in that fatal night.

The drumming in her ears came from the phone in her hand. "If you would like to make a call..." She hung it up. Stared at it, still numb from the shock.

"No message. I'll see him when he gets here."

Of course. That's why he went. To see her.

Directly from my bed! The blow sent her reeling. She clutched at a chair, trying to steady herself against the storm of fury. He had lied to her. Betrayed her. She hated him. Hated the mellow voiced woman on the phone who...

Mel. At last she had surfaced. Had she ever been away?

"Darn! He was supposed to be here last night."

But last night he had been with me... "You, my sexy little temptress!"

Was that what it was? Sex. Nothing more. A one-night stand. No...two.

Have I ever been anything else? The shame of it engulfed her as Lisa's words came back to her... "Seems he was with first one and then another."

But always Mel. If he's meeting her now, he must have been seeing her all along. All those trips to New York or wherever...

The drumming in her ears was now a hammer pounding in her head, a hot stream of anger sizzling through her veins. He had lied to her. Used her! Made her think it was love when it was nothing but...nothing!

The pain of it twisted in her chest, rose like bile in her throat. She wanted to spit it out. To smash something.

With the sweep of one arm she could send it all skittering to the floor...the eggs coagulating on her plate, the coffee cooling in her cup. The fine china, the silver.

Not hers. She had no right.

Moving deliberately and carefully, she dumped the remains of her breakfast into the garbage disposal, rinsed and stacked the dishes, folded the newspaper. Left the kitchen as spotless as she had found it.

In her room, she looked at the tumbled bed, the ashes in the fireplace. Cold.

Not cold enough. The twisting pain, the anger, and the hate burned, a raging fire within her. She walked to the window and pressed her feverish brow against it.

There was something comforting about the sound of rain splashing against the pane, the wind whistling through the trees outside. She watched the raindrops dancing, and forming little riverlets that washed from the patio floor.

Rain. Strange that it should comfort and console. And last night...the drumming of rain against the window had been part of the gentle protective warmth as she lay in his arms. Just as it had drummed on the roof of the *Bluebird* that momentous night when she had first experienced the wonder of love. She had cried out in the throes of erotic fulfillment.

She shook her head, her forehead rubbing against the cool pane. Not love, you fool! Sex.

All right. But the morning she had that flat. The rain had poured down upon her while she leaned against her car, so sick she could hardly stand. He had come down half dressed, held her while she vomited. There's nothing sexy about that!

He had been so kind that day. Had gone to Richmond in her place. Bought her a car. Not just any car, but the Cherokee which she dearly loved. He had said he wanted her to look professional. He had sounded like he was proud of her.

They were compatible, weren't they? All those evenings in the den, the fun they had with the group. She thought...*what you wanted to think!*

Not once had she considered what he wanted.

Face it. You fell in love with him that week on the *Bluebird*. Okay, he was kind. And so much fun. But afterward...did he ever call you?

Oh, no. You called him. Pregnant and begging. You trapped him. And he's been a damn good sport about it.

A gentleman, too. Has he ever taken advantage of the situation? Made any advances?

Oh, no, lady. It was you. You clung to him that night on the *Bluebird*. And last night...remember? The lavender silk with the slits on the sides... "Even a pregnant woman could look sexy, couldn't she?" And when he swallowed the hook, you thought you had him. "He loves me. We're really married."

Your thoughts, Judy. Not his.

She took the note from her pocket and read it again. "Good morning, love" does not say "I love you." Neither does "You're special to me." Any more than "we're compatible" meant we should stay married.

Her thoughts. Not his.

She didn't even have a right to be angry about his

Mel or any other woman. "I'm not asking you to change your life," she had said. "All I'm asking is that you marry me for a few short months."

That was June. This is November.

Time to release him?

He canceled his last meeting. He was so anxious to get home. To her.

She wasn't there when he got in, though it was after five. He lit the fire in the den, paced the floor, and waited. When he heard her car in the garage, he went to meet her in the hall. She had on that kelly green outfit "designed to conceal a bulging middle." Not quite concealed though, even under her jacket. Her face was pale, her hair windblown, and she had the unmistakable stance of a pregnant woman. She looked adorable.

"Hello, love," he said, and moved to take her in his arms.

"Hello, yourself!" She smiled as she stepped quickly past him. "Let me get rid of these things and wash my hands. I know Sadie's waiting dinner."

He waited until she returned, devoid of jacket and purse, hair a little more in order.

"So how did the trip go?" she asked, that bright artificial smile still on her face as again she hurried past him.

"Fine," he said, wondering if she heard him as he followed.

They always ate in the breakfast room when they

were alone. Always talked of impersonal inconsequential things, Sadie joining in as she served them.

So what was different? Why was Judy talking like
a house afire with a kind of forced cheerfulness? It
made him feel damned uncomfortable. Like an un-
wanted guest in his own house!

She might have meant to pass up the den, but he
didn't give her chance. He stopped in front of her,
and held open the door. "We need to talk."

For a minute it seemed she would refuse, but she
finally gave a reluctant nod. She went in and stood
with the chess table between them. She seemed small,
vulnerable, and...hurt?

"What's wrong, Judy?" he asked.

"Wrong? What do you mean?"

"For starters... Why won't you let me touch you?"

The blunt question hit her like a blow. She had not
expected him to be so direct. "Because..." She hesitated. *Because when you touch me I am lost. There's
no reason, no dignity, no Mel. Only you and how
much I want you...any time, anywhere, no matter
what.* "Because...touching leads to...mistakes."

"Mistakes?"

"Like what happened Saturday."

"I thought you enjoyed what happened."

"Sex is always enjoyable," she said, speaking like
the experienced woman she wasn't.

He didn't let her get away with it. "You've made
comparisons to prove it?"

She flushed. "I... Oh, never mind." She shot him

a look. "This isn't a talk. It's an inquisition. Why are you boring in on me like this?"

"I'm just trying to understand. What are you saying?"

"Look, all I'm saying is that we're both human beings, with physical desires that may...may get us into trouble."

"Trouble?"

"You...that is, we got trapped into this make-believe marriage. For both of our sakes we've maintained a pretty good facade. But...it really is just a facade." She ran a tongue over dry lips. He had on that trying-to-figure-her-out look that drove her crazy. Didn't he know she was trying to release him? Without accusations or recriminations. She wasn't screaming at him, scratching out his eyes or that Mel woman's, either, was she! She was just...letting him go, for gosh sake. Because if she didn't... She opened her eyes wide, holding back the tears. "It's time to end this farce. We're getting too close."

"Oh, Judy, listen to me." He came around the table, his arms reaching for her.

"Don't touch me!" If he did, she was lost. Without shame. Glad to be included in his bed hopping.

She did not realize she had screamed, but he did. He stopped short. God, he had never forced himself upon a woman in his life. "Judy, what's wrong? I like getting close. I thought you did, too."

"Well, I don't. I'm sick of this pretense. I'm sick of you." She stopped. Raised horror-stricken eyes to his. "No. I didn't mean that. You've been wonderful. A good sport. I appreciate that. I really do. It's just that I need to get back where I belong. Our agreement was for a few short months. Let's wrap it up, Jake. Please. And can't we talk about this later? I'm so tired."

He moved aside and let her go. He watched the door close behind her. He had never felt so abandoned in his life.

She meant it. She wanted no part of this marriage or him.

Jake was not accustomed to rejection. Quite the other way around. The trouble was, did women like him or his money?

Judy had made it clear that she wanted neither.

Wrapping it up wasn't easy.

Easy to go through the motions. For Judy to immerse herself in work each day. To retire to her room each night, avoiding the den. To avoid being alone with him.

Not easy to dismiss him from her mind. Not to remember his teasing grin when he scored a win at chess...or his blank look of surprise the few times she had managed to capture his king. She missed those quiet companionable moments. Missed the sound of his voice, the laughter, the sharing. Missed the exquisite delight of his arms around her. It was not easy not to want him, whether he was near or away.

He was often away during the days that followed

their last talk in the den. Golfing in Florida. A boat race in Mexico. Business or whatever. She never questioned him about his trips.

Never failed to miss him.

He had to get away. It was not easy to watch her avoiding him.

Not easy not to watch her. As enticing as he had found her that week on the *Bluebird*, it was nothing compared to the way he felt now. She was certainly more beautiful. It was as if she had bloomed with her pregnancy, her hair more golden, a brighter flush to her cheeks, a peaceful serenity in those gorgeous blue eyes. Until lately. Something was disturbing that complacency. Working too hard, he thought. He had called both Charlie and Jim, who was now back at work himself. Suggested that they lighten her load, and left his number to be called in any emergency. Okay, she wanted no part of him. But she was his wife. She was carrying his child, wasn't she?

In any case, he was compelled to care for her, no matter what. He felt closer to her than he had ever felt to any woman. Perhaps it was the confidences they had shared, the intimacy…

The intimacy. Just sex, she had said. Well, he was a damn sight more experienced than she, and he knew it was more than sex!

For you. Not for her.

He didn't believe that. Not the way she had held on to him, called his name over and over again. Loved him, damn it!

In the throes of passion, maybe. But afterward?

"Don't touch me!" she had screamed almost in terror. Oh, she had tried to shield his feelings, apologize... "Two human beings with physical desires. Trapped."

He wouldn't try to hold her against her will. She was right. They had made an agreement. And now, as things stood... Perhaps it was time to wrap it up.

Not easy.

They hadn't realized the strength of the facade they had created...a happily married couple, one of a closely knit group.

The group continued to embrace them, even insisting that Jake cancel any out-of-town commitments for special events...election night in Dover for a midnight toast to Al on his third triumphant victory, Lisa's annual Thanksgiving bash. Christmas dinner at the full Stanford household. And of course there were always the usual routine get-togethers...poker or a spur of the moment dinner at one or another's house.

Perhaps they could have canceled out, and sometimes they did. But most of the time they joined them. They hated to miss the fun. More than fun, Judy thought. Being a part of the group was like having a warm blanket wrapped closely around you, shelter from a winter storm.

It was wrong to feel this way. They should be preparing the group as well as themselves for the coming incompatibility suit. Showing some restraint, or even bickering a bit. But somehow being with the group, sharing the jokes and laughter, seemed to bring them closer, often evoking a smile or glance between Jake and herself, when some remark sparked an intimate memory.

They should have settled on a date, made some preparation for the suit. She should be preparing for the separation, finding an apartment for herself and the baby. She didn't want to return home. Maybe she could take over one of the East End houses in Richmond.

She knew what they should be doing. But somehow they never got around to it.

CHAPTER THIRTEEN

"Judy, it was catching!" Lisa's jubilant voice sang through the telephone.

"Catching?" Judy was puzzled.

"Oh, I'm so glad I bought it. It is a lucky dress. 'Course I don't need to wear it yet, but—"

"Lisa! You're pregnant!"

"Pregnant! With child! In the family way! Two months along, Dr. Lacey says. I couldn't believe it. Like I stopped watching and it slipped up on me."

"Lisa, that's wonderful! I'm so glad!"

"Me, too. And you know what, Judy..." Lisa's voice lowered, almost whispering. "It really was the dress. I've been counting. It must have happened that night. Remember, I went shopping with you and I bought that maternity dress? And I said I wasn't going to try it on for Scot, but I did, and he said I looked so lovely, and started kissing me, and we... Oh, Judy, I'm sure that's the night I got pregnant."

Judy sat down, spooked. Maybe there was something about maternity clothes. That was the night she had shown hers to Jake, and he...they... It was a special night. It was! And now...

"Judy! Judy, are you there?"

163

"Yes." She straightened, trying to get back on track. "I'm listening."

"It was two months ago, wasn't it? Around the first of November...when we went shopping?"

"About."

"See? It was a lucky dress." Lisa chuckled. "More like a lucky night, huh? Anyway, I'm happy. I'm shouting it from the roof. So is Scot. I had to keep him from passing out the cigars now. He wants a boy. I don't care."

"You mean you'll keep it, whichever?"

"You betcha! Oh, Judy, maybe you'll have a boy and I'll have a girl, or vice versa. If so, we could draw up a contract for them to marry when they're eighteen. No, maybe twenty-five. Like in the olden days. What do you think?"

"I think you're crazy." Judy's voice broke. Their children wouldn't even share toddler birthday parties. By that time she'd be...Lord knows where, but definitely out of the "group." She swallowed the lump in her throat. "Haven't you heard? This is today, and today's children are born with minds of their own."

"I know. I'm just being silly because I am so deliriously happy. Scot says I should throw out those baby books and just let our children grow."

Judy laughed. "But you wouldn't be you if you weren't planning, preparing."

"I guess not," Lisa said, sighing.

"Well, I'm doing the planning now."

"Oh?"

"For the party to celebrate that very special long-awaited pregnancy." The least she could do for the woman who had so graciously welcomed her into the group with that rollicking wishing-you-happy party when she had been a nervous, lost, trapped newlywed. "All I want from you is when?" She brushed a tear from her cheek, and managed to nail down a date.

But, before that date, she vowed, she would make some plans for herself. This couldn't go on forever. This pretending to be part of the group...part of Jake. She couldn't stand it. Couldn't stand not touching him when he was near, missing him when he was away. Not hearing him sing in the shower.

How many times had she stood in her own bathroom, an ear pressed to the wall that backed his, just listening? She loved to hear his husky baritone voice, smooth and mellow, rising above the rushing water. Loved the way he would step from the shower, whistling the tune with the same effortless ease. The same joy.

He didn't sing in the shower anymore. She knew, because she always listened.

Because he was unhappy? Anxious to get out of the trap?

He was often away. Did he sing when he was away? With her?

Time to release him. She wanted him happy, wherever he found it.

So, it was for him as well as for herself that, at last, she began to prepare for separation. She selected one of the houses in East End. It was a small house, two bedrooms and only one bath. It was at the end of a cul-de-sac, much safer for children than a through street. Big yard, both front and back, and, unusual for the area, a large brick patio in the back. The patio, like the rest of the house, was, of course, badly in need of repair. But it would be fun to make it beautiful, comfortable, and suited for herself and the baby. She'd add another room and bath. She'd need space for a live-in, since she would have to keep working.

She sat in the Cherokee, drafting sketches for remodeling in her mind, picturing a bright secure house for a smiling blue-eyed baby. But her spirits were as low as the sagging roof. The house looked more dilapidated than ever, immersed, as it was, in soggy drifts of melting snow.

Nothing could be done until spring. She couldn't wait for the house to be fixed. She would have to take an apartment, or spend some time with Jim and Alicia before the house was ready.

Jim and Alicia had taken off for Florida for a month, partly for Jim's health, but also because construction was so slow he could be spared. Judy was glad they were away. She was reluctant to tell them of the coming divorce. She sighed. It was going to be as hard to tell people of their separation as it had been to spring the sudden marriage.

As she put the Cherokee in gear and started to pull away, she caught sight of the forlorn For Sale sign that had flopped over. It reminded her that all their houses were for sale. She didn't want this one sold out from under her. She had to tell someone. Charlie.

She found him overseeing some cabinet work in a house that, thankfully, had been insulated before winter set in. He was glad to take a coffee break.

"I'm taking number ten on Brady Street off the list," she said. "I want to keep it."

"Oh? Why?"

"For myself. I…" She kept her eyes on the steaming mug of coffee wrapped in her hands. "Look, I don't want this spread around, but I'm planning…thinking of leaving Jake."

She felt, rather than saw his start of surprise. "Oh, no! That is, I thought…" He stopped. "I'm sorry. He's been down here a few times, you know, and I thought… Well, he seems like a pretty decent guy."

"Oh, he is. He is!" She didn't want anyone to think he wasn't. "He's more than decent. He's kind, thoughtful, generous, and—" Now it was she who came to an abrupt stop. She had to give some reason. "It's nothing to do with him. I mean the kind of guy he is. It's…well, a different lifestyle. I don't seem to fit in."

Her spirits were low, but they would not dampen Lisa's party. Judy was determined that it would be as festive and as much fun as her welcome-to-the-gang had been.

"You won't be out of town then, will you?" she asked Jake two weeks before the affair.

"I'll make it back. Wouldn't miss it! Scot would kill me if I passed him up for golf. Besides, Lisa's pretty special to me. She's on cloud nine, isn't she?"

"Yes." Judy turned away. How different had been her own reaction. How her life had been so disrupted.

Well, she wouldn't let what happened almost seven months ago cast a cloud on Lisa's happiness! It might be a goodbye party for herself as well as a celebration, but it would be a bang-up goodbye! A bang-up celebration!

She planned carefully, selecting the right place settings and color scheme—the neutral yellow—and bought balloons and other decorations. She stayed home from work the day of the party to help Sadie get everything ready.

"Get off that chair, child!" Sadie scolded three hours before the party was to begin. "You could fall doing all that climbing and reaching. Besides you've already got enough balloons hanging all over the place."

Judy gave a sheepish grin, and obediently stepped down. She knew she was overdoing it. After all, it was just another get-together for the tightly knit little group. Special because it would be her last. Of course nobody but she knew that. Not even Jake.

Where was Jake? He had promised to cut short his Florida trip, said he would be here. But it was now three…no, two hours and a half before. She kept listening for his car. Kept wondering if he had been delayed by something or someone. Mel? She couldn't bear it if he weren't here.

"Why don't you go up and take a short rest?" Sadie asked. "You've got time, and Lord knows you need one."

Judy assented. There was nothing else to be done, and no need to keep watching. Either Jake would be there or he wouldn't.

She had started upstairs when she heard his car. She hurried on up, not wanting him to see the relief and pleasure that would surely show on her face. He was here. Now she could relax, maybe sleep a little.

Only she couldn't. Too excited and nervous. She lay on her bed, listening to the sounds in the next room.

Jake moving around. Unpacking? Not whistling.

She kept turning and twisting, unable to get comfortable. She was glad when it was time to dress. She was in the shower when she was gripped by a pain in the lower back that made her gasp and lean against the shower wall. Kind'a like a menstrual cramp, she thought, breathing easier as the pain subsided. Well, it surely couldn't be that. Sore muscles. Sadie was right, she'd done too much getting up and down. She lingered in the shower, letting the hot water pour over her tired muscles.

She slipped on the lavender dress and anxiously surveyed herself in the mirror. It was all right. She had gained, but not too much. She was glad. She wanted to wear it. It was symbolic of the good times.

She thought about that. To be honest, there hadn't been any bad times. No squabbles or disagreements. They had lived together comfortably, to all appearances, a normal happily married couple.

Her mouth twisted. If they really had been a normal happily married couple, there would have been a hell of a squabble. She would have raised the roof about that Mel woman! Her heart would have ached as it did now. She would probably have left him as she was going to do anyway.

Oh, well... She wouldn't think about that. On with the party.

She put on lipstick, brushed her hair, and went downstairs. The gang would be arriving soon.

"Hey, hey! This is going to be one grand affair!" Jake was looking at her decorations.

She was looking at him. She hadn't expected him to be down. Hadn't been prepared for the sight of his sun-bleached hair and deeply tanned skin. Just as he had looked last summer on the *Bluebird*. Had his eyes squinted in the Florida sun? Had Mel been with him? Judy felt the jealous pang, even as her heart spun with joy. He was here.

"It looks great, Judy. Scot and Lisa will be so pleased. Thank you," he said, as if she had done it for him.

Had she done it for him? To prove that they belonged together, that... She grimaced, feeling that funny pain again!

"What's the matter?"

"Nothing." She wasn't going to let a silly muscle cramp spoil her party. "This doesn't look right," she said, picking at a flower arrangement. "Oh, there's the doorbell. Will you get it?"

The party was festive and fun, typical of all their gatherings, everybody talking at once, poking fun at each other. Only, to Judy, it seemed to go on and on forever. Perhaps she had overdone it. She felt so tired. She tried not to let it show, joining in the laughter and jests, most of which were focused on Scot and Lisa who reveled in it. Scot was booking bets on the baby's sex.

"Those who are right will collect," he said. "And those who guessed wrong will pay." He kept looking at Lisa as if he could eat her alive. And no wonder, Judy thought. Lisa was lovelier than ever, glowing with happiness.

As Judy watched, waves of hurt and envy spun through her, curled in upon themselves, and settled in her chest, a fiery ball of resentment. Nobody had been happy when she got pregnant. Nobody.

Good Lord! She was envious. And she was taking it out on the happy couple before her. It wasn't their fault that she had gotten herself into this tangled mess. What was wrong with her? That pain maybe, that nipped her in the back every now and then. And Jake, the way he was watching her with a kind of critical appraisal that made her feel anxious. Everything was going well, wasn't it? Everyone seemed happy.

"All right!" she called out. "Get ready. I made the

dessert myself!'' Sadie brought it in, and she served the fluffy slices of lemon meringue pie. A huge success. All the men took seconds.

"Superb!" Jake declared, and blew her a kiss from across the table.

Judy flushed. The kiss and the compliment flowed through her like an intoxicating glass of potent wine.

The party was winding down with coffee and brandy in the living room when the talk reverted to Jake's Florida trip and golf.

"Lucky guy!" Scot said. "Basking in the sun while we working guys slaved away, cooped in an office, bending over a desk."

"Oh? Weren't you in London last month?" Jake asked. "Seems to me you're always going somewhere. Bermuda or the French Riviera, or wherever an extremely pleasant business-write-off conference can be conveniently arranged."

"Not much difference between a conference room and a desk," Scot declared. "It's still work."

"Must be tough," Jake said in mock sympathy.

"Well, we don't get a suntan while perfecting our golf stroke. I've been trying to tell you, my boy, there's a difference between us nine-to-five types and you rich loafers."

Judy's ire rose as the usual banter continued. She didn't care who won their stupid games. But she didn't like their saying that Jake always won because he did nothing but play. He did much more. He was so easygoing and modest about all the really marvelous things he did, that nobody noticed. Too easy-going. She wanted to shake him. Sitting there like a bump on a log, just grinning, while Scot, Al, and even Stan dumped on him.

"Must be nice," Scot said, as if in conclusion. "Just sit back and clip your coupons while we work to keep the economy going."

"Stop saying that!" She was as surprised as the others to find herself on her feet, fists clenched. "Jake's not just a playboy. He may not sit at a desk, but he contributes more to the world's economy than a lot of people who do. You said it yourself. That merger he stopped saved twenty-five hundred jobs. Jobs of people with families to feed, children to educate. You better be glad he's rich. Because he's kind, and thoughtful, and generous, and cares about people. He's like a maestro waving his wealth like a magic wand to promote this idea or that. Not just for big corporations, but for little people who have big ideas and no backing...like the engineer who might develop electric cars and rid us of pollution, or the two young boys now running a rafting traveling agency. If it wasn't for Jake, they'd still be selling hamburgers instead of building a company that's hiring other people.

"And I'll tell you something else. You better be glad he plays. He met that engineer on a golf course and those two boys at a basketball game. Because he listens...even to a teenage boy who wants to get on the school basketball team. Jake tutored him in algebra and…'' The sharp constriction made her gasp. She placed a hand on her back and paused, suddenly aware that everyone was staring at her.

What had come over her! Spieling off about Jake to these people who knew him far better than she, who were just joking anyway. What must they think of her? All up in a huff.

She gave a sheepish grin, feeling absolutely ridiculous.

''Okay, guys. Lecture is over. Just want to make sure you appreciate my husband.'' She glanced at Jake. He had been lounging on the floor before the fire, but now he was sitting straight up, staring at her. She lowered her eyes, sat down, wishing she could call back her words.

She was relieved to hear Stan laugh. ''Guess that'll learn you not to bad-mouth Jake when Judy is around.''

''Right,'' Lisa said. ''I'm glad you're here, Judy. I've been trying to keep them off Jake's back.''

Judy smiled, feeling a little better, glad they were taking it lightly.

''Didn't mean no harm, Mrs. Mason.'' Scot gave an obsequious nod. ''Just have to bring him down a peg or two every now and then. He does everything so damn well.''

Judy smiled at him. ''Oh, Scot…'' She broke off as another pain hit her. Not muscle cramps. It wasn't time. Not quite seven months. God! Was she going to lose her baby?

CHAPTER FOURTEEN

THE rest of the evening was a blur to Judy. But she kept with it, laughing and joking with the rest, ignoring the recurring spasms. Denying what was happening. It was too early. She wasn't going to lose her baby. She wasn't!

How did you know? Timing...when the interval between pains was shorter. These were at least a half hour apart, maybe more. But they wouldn't stay that way for two months. Only two more months! "Don't let go," she silently pleaded to the babe within her. "Hold on. Please."

They were leaving. She stood with Jake to smile her goodbyes and receive their thanks. Relieved. She would go up and lie down and the pains would go away.

"Give me a few minutes, will you, Jake?" she heard Al say. "I need some input about that bill I'm introducing."

"Sure," Jake said. "Why don't you and Ada stay the night? In the morning we'll—"

"No can do. Committee meeting first thing tomorrow. We'll have to get back to Dover tonight."

"Damn it, Al," Jake grumbled. "You want everything done yesterday.'' But he assented, as Judy knew he would. ''Okay, come on in the den.''

He never refuses to listen, Judy thought as she and Ada started to follow. But Jake turned to her. ''You're tired, Judy. Go on up. Ada won't mind.''

''Of course not,'' Ada said. ''I know you need your rest. Go on up and I'll stay with the guys and make sure Al doesn't keep Jake too long. Great party, honey,'' she added, kissing Judy's cheek.

Judy went to her room, relieved. But Jake's curt dismissal had registered. Reinforced the fact that she had embarrassed him tonight, when she had taken Scot on. Scot, who had kidded with him like that all of their lives! She, the outsider, didn't understand. Didn't belong.

She kicked off her shoes in a sudden burst of anger. It wasn't all my fault. I didn't plan this baby any more than you did! I— A sharp spasm reminded her. What had she been saying?

''I didn't mean it,'' she said aloud. Her hands flew to cradle her unborn child. ''I do want you. Oh, please…hold on. I don't want to lose you. You're all I have…all I'll ever have.'' She paced the floor, her mind groping for what could have gone wrong. She had religiously followed the doctor's instructions, taken the test. They hadn't been able to determine the sex because of the baby's position, but they had assured her that it was healthy. So what was wrong?

''I didn't mean it,'' she whispered. ''I love you. You were conceived in love, that night, the most wonderful night of my life. Do you remember? On the *Bluebird*...'' She stood perfectly still. The *Bluebird*. If he were there, where he was conceived in love, would he remember? Would everything be all right?

She slipped on her pumps, grabbed her coat, and silently left the house.

Snowflakes were falling by the time she got the Cherokee on the highway. No matter. The roads were still passable. And she knew the *Bluebird* would be waiting. Jake didn't sail during the winter months, but he often went there to relax. Sims always kept it in readiness. She would get the key from him. But when she called Sims, there was no answer. Would he be on the boat? She didn't know. She only felt this compulsion to get there. To let her child remember that he was conceived in love.

Please let Sims be there, she prayed as she made her way across the parking lot. Thank you, she murmured, as she stepped aboard and saw a light shining inside the cabin. She pressed the bell and waited. A long time. Maybe Sims wasn't there, but had just left the light on. She must have been crazy to come here.

She heard light footsteps. A cautious voice. A feminine voice. "Jake? Is that you?"

In spite of the cold, she felt hot as rage began to simmer. "Not Jake," she said. "Jake's wife. Judy Mason." She had a right, didn't she? She was his wife, wasn't she!

The door was opened immediately. "Oh, do come in."

Judy stepped inside, staring at the woman who stared back at her. Beautiful sea green eyes, small upturned nose and perfectly shaped lips that also tilted upward. A cloud of red hair tumbled to her shoulders and she had a delicate ethereal look, even enveloped in the heavy blue terry-cloth robe that Judy had borrowed that night.

Judy felt awkward, like a wobbly inflated balloon, only heavier.

Neither spoke, but Judy could read the question in the sea green eyes: What in the world are you doing here this time of night? Spying on Jake?

"I'm not—" She stopped, realizing she was answering a question that had not been spoken. "It's just... I'm sorry." She had been wrong to come. She had no right...to be where she did not belong. Hadn't she promised not to interfere with his life? "You're Mel," she said, and barely noticed the almost imperceptible nod. This was Mel, who had been part of his life before her. Whom he would have married had he not gotten trapped?

"I'm sorry," she said again. "I'll go." She didn't belong here...where Mel was waiting.

"Don't be ridiculous! You shouldn't be out in this weather. And in your condition. Whatever possessed you to—" She broke off, as puzzlement gave way to compassion. "Look, I don't know what's wrong, but it's snowing out there! Or, hadn't you noticed?" The twinkle in her green eyes seemed to ease the tension, and Judy numbly obeyed her command to "Come into the galley and let me fix you a hot drink. You must be freezing.''

She was freezing. And feeling like a fool, sitting in the little breakfast booth, hugging her coat around her, watching Mel fill a mug of milk and place it in the microwave with the easy familiarity of one who belonged. I must be crazy, Judy thought. To come tearing down here just because the baby... She drew a quick breath, struck by the realization. The pains had stopped. Or had she been too distracted to notice?

She felt the little kick in her stomach, like a nudge of reassurance. No spasm. She had been right to come. Everything was back to normal, wasn't it?

''Good heavens, your shoes are soaked.''

Judy, still grappling with the possible miracle, watched as Mel knelt to remove the lavender pumps. The bright red hair fell across her face like a halo as she began to massage Judy's feet with warm gentle hands. Like a ministering angel.

She didn't talk like an angel. ''That was a damn fool stunt to pull. Trudging through the snow in these. And at this time of night! Did you have a fight? Does Jake know where the hell you are? Of course not or you wouldn't be here!'' The microwave buzzed, and she got up to retrieve the hot milk. ''Chocolate?'' she asked.

Judy nodded, feeling very strange. How could she be so comfortable, while Jake's love waited on her? She could see why Jake loves her. She's so beautiful. So kind. Acting like we're the best of friends, and it's perfectly normal for me to burst in and get her out of bed in the middle of the night. She hasn't even asked me why! She's just been...kind.

"This will warm you up," Mel said, handing her the drink.

"Thank you." Judy wrapped her cold hands around the mug, and drank. The hot sweet liquid did warm her, and somehow managed to soothe her shattered nerves, enable her to think. She hadn't had one single pain since arriving. Everything was going to be all right. She would have her baby. And Jake...Jake would have Mel. Beautiful, kind Mel. Tears burned in her eyes, but she managed to hold them back. Mel would make him happy.

She had to be sure. "You and Jake..." She hesitated. How did you ask your husband's mistress if she really loved him? The only straight way was straight out. She took the plunge. "You do love him?"

Mel seem surprised by the question, but answered readily. "More than anyone on earth."

It hit her like a quick jab to the heart. Why? She wanted Mel to love him, didn't she? Wanted him to be happy.

"Yes, Jake is very special to me." At the moment, Mel seemed wrapped in a world of her own. Elbows on the table, chin in her hands, eyes staring into space. "If he hadn't come... He literally saved my life."

"Oh?" Judy was touched by the flash of pain in those green eyes. And curious. "What happened?"

Mel turned to her, as if suddenly remembering she

was there. "Oh, damn! Why did I bring that up? It happened six years ago when I was a young and very foolish eighteen. I had run away from home, you see, and had too much pride to go back." She picked up Judy's cup, stood to rinse it in the sink and put it in the dishwasher, talking all the time. 'I was in a bad way and Jake came and got me."

Like he had rescued her, Judy thought. "Did he bring you here?"

"Here?"

"To the *Bluebird*, I mean?"

"Gosh no! He took me home and talked some sense into me." Mel stood with her hands on the sink now and the humor was back in her eyes. "Strange you should ask though. Jake always had a boat and we had always done a lot of sailing before then. But...well, I was having a hell of a time, getting over Di...over what had happened. If Jake hadn't dragged me out, made me go sailing...I guess that was what really gave me the courage and strength to bounce back."

"Yes. A sail can put the wind in you." It had done that for her, Judy thought.

"Right. I'm as much of a sailor as Jake, but too much of a rolling stone to own a boat. Jake's boat is a haven for me whenever I'm home. I just got in this evening and headed straight for the *Bluebird*. I tell myself it's because this is nearer the airport." Mel gave a rueful smile. "Really it's because the *Bluebird* is more a home to me than where I live. Even when we can't go sailing.''

''I see,'' Judy said. It sounded as if Mel and Jake went a long way back. ''You and Jake have been close for a long time then?''

''All our lives. Plenty of cousins in the Mason clan, but Jake and I were closer than most. Possibly because our mothers were closer than most sisters. He's four years older than I, but more like a brother than a cousin.''

''You're not...?'' She tried to absorb it. Joy! Disbelief. Confusion. ''You're cousins?''

''Of course. Don't tell me he's never mentioned me?''

''No,'' Judy cried, stung by a sensation wavering between joy and anger. Just let me borrow your clothes. Let me go crazy with jealousy, thinking—

''The closemouthed jerk! He didn't tell me about you, either. Not until a couple of months ago.''

Because it wasn't a real marriage, Judy thought. Maybe he was waiting until it was over. ''What did he tell you?'' Judy held her breath. Had he confided to this sister/cousin that he had been trapped?

''Not much. Just that he was married and you were pregnant.''

''Oh.'' Judy remembered their wedding day, Jake's, ''I've got friends and relations, too. Damn if I'm going to look trapped.'' Why did she feel so relieved that he hadn't told Mel?

''Of course I only saw him for a hot minute. We

both were in New York on business, and by the time we got together, I was about to depart for Japan.''

"Japan?" Judy murmured. But she was thinking of New York and that phone call. "I'm Mel. I'll see him when he gets here."

"I've been in Japan since last March. That's why we've never met before."

"I see," Judy said, still thinking of the phone call that had left her devastated. She had withdrawn. Not Jake. He had reached out to take her in his arms. She could still see his face when she cried, "Don't touch me!" How could she unsay it? Make him know how much she loved him.

"Hadn't we better call Jake?" Mel asked. "He must be out of his mind, wondering where you are."

"No!" Judy cried, remembering how he had looked at her tonight. She had done everything wrong. At least he wouldn't have to know she had come here. "He doesn't...wouldn't..."

"Doesn't know? Or wouldn't be worried?"

"Both. I mean neither!" How could she convince Mel without explaining? "We don't...we sleep in separate rooms, because of the baby," she said rapidly. "I'd not like him to know I've been out. If I go back now—"

"The hell you will! Jake would kill me if I let you out! We're both tired. Let's go to bed."

She knew Mel was right. She might not make it back through the snow. Might not be able to slip back in as silently as she had left. And she was so tired.

But for a long time she lay awake. This time in the big bed in Jake's quarters, his things around her. "It's still the *Bluebird*," she told her baby. "This is your daddy's bed. Everything is going to be all right." But even as she said it, she wondered. Could she make Jake know that she loved him? Did he want to know?

Did he love her?

What damn fools we mortals are, Melody Sands thought, as she retreated to her own cabin. We don't know how to hold on to a good thing when we've got it any more than we know how to turn it loose when it's rotten.

She had held on to Dirk, hadn't she? Even after he had sold out on her for a measly fifty thousand dollars. She had loved him so much. The handsome, virile, daring, ski instructor who had taught her to soar over the snowy slopes. Who had held her in his arms and talked of undying love.

She had believed in him, would have gone with him to hell and back without one damn penny. She could still see the drab motel room where she had waited and waited. Until Jake had come.

It had taken Jake a long time to convince her not to hate her father. It was Dirk who had run like a weasel when faced with the loss of her inheritance if they carried out their plans to marry.

Rotten. But it had taken her a long time to get over him. Maybe she wasn't over him yet, she admitted.

She couldn't trust any man, couldn't...wouldn't dare to fall in love again.

Damn it, why was she thinking of that! She ought to be thinking of Jake.

Did Jake know what he had? That woman really loved him. She had seen the astonishment and joy when she learned they were cousins, not lovers. But, before she knew, she had asked, "Do you love him?" As if her main concern was his happiness. Greater love than this was damn hard to come up with!

Still, something was wrong. Judy here, alone, at a time like this. And... "We sleep in separate rooms...because of the baby."

Bull! Something was wrong as hell.

Maybe Jake didn't love her.

Maybe he didn't know what a good thing he had.

Anyway, she had not promised not to call him. She picked up the phone.

Judy awakened out of a deep sleep when her husband shook her gently, "Judy, honey, are you all right? The baby?"

"Yes," she muttered, still a little dazed. "I'm fine. The baby...both of us."

He gripped her shoulders and glared down at her. "Then what the hell are you doing here? Sneaking off. Why? Driving me crazy. When I went up and found you weren't there, that your bed hadn't been slept in. I—"

"You came to my room?" To me? she wondered, a tiny hope springing to life.

"Damn right. Tonight, when you lit into Scot—"

"I'm sorry. I know you were mad."

"Mad? I was loving it. That guy's been picking on me since kindergarten."

"I know. But he was joking and you knew he was joking. It was so stupid for me to—"

"To come to my defense? I loved it, I tell you. The things you said...well, it made me think you liked me a little. You've been so standoffish lately, I thought—"

"Oh, Jake, I didn't mean to be. I was just so scared, so hurt. That night before you went to New York was so...so..." She flung her arms around him, hiding her face against his chest. "So wonderful. I thought everything was right between us."

"So did I, sweet. So did I." He brushed back her hair, kissed her forehead. "What happened?"

She told him, her face still buried against him. She poured out all the doubt, the frustration. "I love you so much, and I thought you didn't love me. I had to pull away."

"Sweetheart, I've loved you since...well, maybe not the first time I saw you in all that wedding finery. Certainly after that week on the *Bluebird*."

"You didn't act like it. Especially when I turned up pregnant."

"I know. I had my suspicions, too. It's a good thing you did turn up pregnant. I might never have known

how much you mean to me, how much I love you.''
He tilted her chin, kissed her tenderly. "You know
something else? I'm pretty darn grateful to a guy
named Ben Cruz. If he had married you...if he hadn't
taken off...Christ! Wonder where he is? I ought to
send him another check.''

"Oh, you! I think you've paid him enough.'' She
laughed, but she felt rather grateful to Ben herself.

"Hey, wait a minute,'' he said, sitting up and re-
garding her with stern eyes. "You haven't explained
why you came down here, and drove me crazy. I
looked all over the house, woke up Sadie before I
found your car was gone. I was halfway to Elmwood
when Mel caught me on the car phone. Why did you
take off and for here of all places?''

"Because this is where our baby was conceived,''
she said, grinning.

"And?''

"Well, I had a few labor pains. False,'' she added
quickly, seeing his alarm. "But I was so scared. I
thought you didn't want me, and I thought the baby
felt rejected because...well, remember how at first...
I thought if I came here, he, or she, would remember
that it was conceived in love and wouldn't leave me.''

"Oh, honey,'' he said, rocking her gently back and
forth.

"It worked,'' she said. "The baby knew. The pains
stopped as soon as I got here.''

"Smart baby,'' he said. "To know what we didn't

know ourselves. But we know it now, don't we? Wherever we are, on the *Bluebird* or off, our baby will be wrapped in love. Our love.''

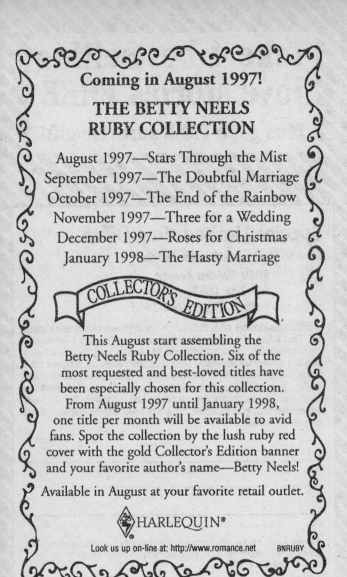

Take 4 bestselling love stories FREE

Plus get a FREE surprise gift!

Special Limited-time Offer

Mail to Harlequin Reader Service®

3010 Walden Avenue
P.O. Box 1867
Buffalo, N.Y. 14240-1867

YES! Please send me 4 free Harlequin Romance® novels and my free surprise gift. Then send me 6 brand-new novels every month, which I will receive months before they appear in bookstores. Bill me at the low price of $2.67 each plus 25¢ delivery and applicable sales tax if any*. That's the complete price and a savings of over 10% off the cover prices—quite a bargain! I understand that accepting the books and gift places me under no obligation ever to buy any books. I can always return a shipment and cancel at any time. Even if I never buy another book from Harlequin, the 4 free books and the surprise gift are mine to keep forever.

116 BPA A3UK

Name	(PLEASE PRINT)	
Address	Apt. No.	
City	State	Zip

This offer is limited to one order per household and not valid to present Harlequin Romance® subscribers. *Terms and prices are subject to change without notice. Sales tax applicable in N.Y.

UROM-696 ©1990 Harlequin Enterprises Limited

Free Gift Offer

With a Free Gift proof-of-purchase
from any Harlequin® book, you can receive
a beautiful cubic zirconia pendant.

This stunning marquise-shaped stone is a genuine cubic
zirconia—accented by an 18" gold tone necklace.
(Approximate retail value $19.95)

Send for yours today...
compliments of ◆ HARLEQUIN®

To receive your free gift, a cubic zirconia pendant, send us one original proof-of-purchase, photocopies not accepted, from the back of any Harlequin Romance®, Harlequin Presents®, Harlequin Temptation®, Harlequin Superromance®, Harlequin Love & Laughter®, Harlequin Intrigue®, Harlequin American Romance®, or Harlequin Historicals® title available at your favorite retail outlet, together with the Free Gift Certificate, plus a check or money order for $1.65 U.S./$2.15 CAN. (do not send cash) to cover postage and handling, payable to Harlequin Free Gift Offer. We will send you the specified gift. Allow 6 to 8 weeks for delivery. Offer good until March 31, 1998, or while quantities last. Offer valid in the U.S. and Canada only.

Free Gift Certificate

Name: _____

Address: _____

City: _____ State/Province: _____ Zip/Postal Code: _____

Mail this certificate, one proof-of-purchase and a check or money order for postage and handling to: HARLEQUIN FREE GIFT OFFER 1998. In the U.S.: 3010 Walden Avenue, P.O. Box 9071, Buffalo NY 14269-9057. In Canada: P.O. Box 604, Fort Erie, Ontario L2Z 5X3.

FREE GIFT OFFER   084-KEZ

ONE PROOF-OF-PURCHASE
To collect your fabulous FREE GIFT, a cubic zirconia pendant, you must include this original proof-of-purchase for each gift with the properly completed Free Gift Certificate.

084-KEZR2